WAITING
FOR AMY

A PILGRIMAGE INTO THE MIND

By

Michael Small

To my grandchildren, John and Ted.

CONTENTS

ACKNOWLEDGMENTS

My sincere thanks to Jill, Jo and Anton for reading the drafts, suggesting improvements, and giving me moral support.

My special thanks to Yanina for her professional help and expertise in the publication process.

INTRODUCTION

The Camino de Santiago (in English, the Way of St James) is descriptive of a number of traditional pilgrim routes across northern Spain leading to the great cathedral of Santiago de Compostela, where the relics of St James the Apostle are enshrined.

Nowadays people come from all over the world to walk the Camino de Santiago, and the most popular route for modern pilgrims begins at St-Jean-Pied-de-Port in the French Pyrenees and follows a way indicated by yellow arrows and scallop shell waymarks until Santiago de Compostela – a distance of some 800 kilometres.

Whereas such pilgrimages in the Middle Ages were undertaken strictly for spiritual reasons, modern followers of the yellow arrows often have more secular motives…

1. FROM THE BEGINNING

He watched the goosebumps forming on her bare arms. This could be a sign of sexual arousal, of course, but it was much more likely to be an indication of fear, as she fumbled with the seatbelt.

As his glance moved up from her arms to her youthful face, their eyes met and he gave her what he hoped was a reassuring smile. He would have liked to hold her hand but resisted the temptation. You don't take the hand of a complete stranger just because she is sitting next to you on a budget airline flight. He had a feeling of déjà vu, recalling a similar occasion nearly forty years earlier when he had done just that, with someone he hardly knew. He quickly put it out of his mind. It was not something he wanted to remember.

"Cabin crew, take your seats ready for landing." The voice of the pilot was calm and controlled.

Wade checked his own seatbelt again and tried to

relax, but his heart was beating faster. Even though he had flown many times over the years this part of the flight always made him nervous, and as they neared Santander from the sea it quickly became apparent that it wouldn't be a comfortable landing.

Conditions were very bumpy after they crossed the Spanish coast and flew over the rocky hills surrounding the city, with the plane sometimes lurching to one side or simply dropping like a stone without any warning. There were stifled screams from some passengers, while others, white-faced and with wide staring eyes, clung grimly to the armrests. Wade was one of those who suffered in silence, trying to suppress all outward signs of emotion, a characteristic he had assumed and cultivated ever since the breakup of his marriage some years previously.

He glanced anxiously through the porthole. They appeared to be quite near the ground now and it was possible to pick out individual houses and cars in the streets below. As they continued the final approach to the airport prior to landing, the aircraft was pitching violently. Then suddenly there was a roar of engine noise and the plane climbed steeply before turning back towards the sea.

"We're going to try the landing again," the senior flight attendant announced somewhat hesitantly on the intercom.

Wade's stomach tightened. Was his journey going to end before it had really begun? Maybe he should pray, but to whom? The thought flashed through his mind: *I'm not ready to die yet – not before I've even started my pilgrimage.*

3

His unspoken prayers were soon answered, because almost immediately there came a cheerful announcement from the pilot informing them that, due to worsening weather conditions in Santander, they had been diverted to Bilbao airport, further up the coast. The pilot apologised for any inconvenience this might cause, but Wade was pleased because Bilbao was a step on the way to St-Jean-Pied-de-Port and the real start of his pilgrimage – the Camino de Santiago de Compostela, the centuries-old pilgrims' way right across northern Spain to the cathedral of Santiago. Was this diversion some kind of sign from above? Was he being given a final chance to regain the faith in God that he had felt in his youth and be ready to meet his maker when the time came?

Their landing at Bilbao airport went without incident and Wade was soon waiting for a bus into the city. He was a tall, grey-haired man of medium build, and just slightly overweight. He had a good complexion for his age, and it wasn't until you got close that you noticed the lines of care in his face and a touch of sadness in his eyes. The late autumn sun was shining brightly and beads of sweat were trickling down his forehead. He mopped his brow with a tissue. It was much warmer here than in England, so he removed his jacket and strapped it to his backpack, which he had propped up against a bench near the bus stop.

He looked hard at his backpack, which was stuffed to capacity, hoping that he had not forgotten anything vital. There were a few non-essentials he would have liked to bring with him, including the book he was currently reading, but there just wasn't any space for luxuries. So, he had reluctantly left Paulo Coelho's *Pilgrimage* lying unfinished on the kitchen table. It was a mysterious book, a spiritual quest, and Wade felt that it somehow related to his own journey. Maybe he would understand it better when he got back home again.

He had little time to reflect before the next bus arrived. Here he was, aged sixty-nine, finally getting out of the rut and setting off on an adventure of self-discovery. Though he quite often flew from London to Frankfurt, to keep in touch with family and friends, this was the first time in years that he'd gone anywhere new, or done anything different.

The city bus was crowded with people who had come in on the same flight as Wade, most of them concerned about how they were going to get back to Santander. He didn't have this problem because he had already booked a room for the night in Bilbao when he was planning the journey. His accommodation was located near the bus station, and he would travel from there to Bayonne the next day, before finally taking a train to St-Jean-Pied-de-Port. Even so, when he alighted from the bus he was a little nervous. He was alone in a strange city, very conscious that he had a vocabulary of about twenty words of Spanish and wary as a zoo animal being released into the wild for the first time.

Wade found the Pension Arias easily enough and after freshening up he ventured cautiously out to explore the city, or at least that part of it which lay nearby. He walked a few blocks before daring to buy a snack at a kiosk in the street and then, on his way back, he went into a small bar near the pension. It was early evening and there were no other customers yet.

The young woman behind the counter greeted him with a friendly smile and looked at him expectantly, waiting for his order. Wade wanted a glass of red wine, but he suddenly realised that he didn't even know enough Spanish to ask for it. He hesitated for a moment before speaking.

"Er... vino roso por favor?" It really was more of a question than an order for a drink.

The barmaid smiled again and looked at him quizzically. Then she brought two bottles from behind the bar and placed them on the counter in front of him. One was a bottle of rosé and the other a red wine.

"Vino rosado... y vino tinto," she said, showing him the bottles in turn.

Wade pointed at the red wine. "Ah! ...Vino tinto, por favor." He sat at a table with his red wine and speculated on how the barmaid could have guessed that he wasn't a rosé drinker.

*

The following afternoon, a slow train meandered up the Nive Valley to St-Jean-Pied-de-Port, where Wade and just a few other backpack-carrying passengers alighted at the small station. Although it was late October, and the main Camino season had ended, the weather was warm enough for Wade to break into a sweat as he walked from the station into the ancient Basque town, nestling at the foot of the French Pyrenees. He was excited. This would be the beginning of his pilgrimage, an event he had been looking forward to and planning for the past several months. Now it was becoming reality.

First of all, he searched for the pilgrims' information office to pick up his Credencial (or pilgrim's passport) a document that would enable him to stay at official hostels along the way. It was cooler in the office and he was glad to take off his backpack for a few minutes. As he waited for his turn he chose one of the scallop shells on sale – the pilgrim's badge – which he would attach to his backpack later.

"The weather will be fine tomorrow," the middle-aged lady in charge of the front desk told him, "so you can walk the Route Napoléon to Roncesvalles, but be sure to take plenty of water with you because the springs on the mountain dried up during the summer and the pilgrims' hostel in Orrison has closed until next year."

Wade had read about this route in his guidebook. It had a reputation for being one of the more strenuous stages of the whole Camino, but also one of the most beautiful. He had hoped to be able to break this first stage at Orrison, but it now looked like he would have to walk the whole way across the Pyrenean mountains to Roncesvalles in one go.

"Merci Madame, and can you recommend a hostel for tonight?"

"Yes, the Refuge Municipal is for pilgrims only. It's just a few metres up the street."

2. BODY

Wade had not slept well. There had been a storm in the night, with lightning flashes and the rumble of thunder. Quite apart from this, he was not used to sleeping in a dormitory – certainly not a mixed one. In spite of arriving early enough to be able to grab a bottom bunk, the excitement, the expectations of the journey and the snoring of his fellow pilgrims had all combined to keep him awake for much of the night.

He was the last pilgrim to leave the hostel, not so much because he got up later than anyone else, but more because it took him longer to get ready than any of the other pilgrims who had spent the night there. When planning this trip he had become obsessed with the need to keep the size and weight of his backpack down to a minimum, and there was absolutely no spare capacity. He had a great deal of trouble cramming everything into the backpack and then, when he thought he had succeeded, he noticed his toiletries bag lying on his bunk. How had he missed that?

"Shit!" he muttered to himself as he tackled the packing problem once again.

It was barely eight o'clock and quite dark outside as he walked down the largely deserted, narrow, cobbled street towards the ancient gateway at the foot of the town and the start of the Route Napoléon. With the dawn just breaking and other pilgrims appearing out of the gloom, also following the marked way, he began the steady climb up the gravel track.

The sun rose over the high, distant peaks and the dark folds of the nearby hills turned to a lighter green with the promise of a fine day. Wade was feeling stronger now, enjoying the late October sunshine and the stunning mountain scenery of the Pyrenees stretching to the horizon. He walked alone until he reached Orrison, where a number of other pilgrims were resting near the fountain opposite the hostel.

He was greeted with big smiles and, "Hola!" from a group of Koreans – a girl and three young men. None of them looked more than about twenty-five years old. There was also an older man, very tall, wearing a baseball cap, and with the physique of an ex-sportsman gone to seed. He was probably from the USA.

"Hi," said the tall man, who looked to be just a few years younger than Wade. He was standing with an empty water bottle in his hand. "Nothing to drink here, I'm afraid. If all the springs are dry, we'll be dehydrated by the time we get to Roncesvalles. By the way, my name's Matt. I'm from Chicago."

"I'm Wade, from London." They shook hands and shortly afterwards set off together up the mountain road.

The higher they climbed, the more open were the views, with the soft green slopes of the surrounding hills being set against a background of majestic, brown-grey, rocky peaks on the distant horizon. Up here, above the shelter of the valleys, a strong wind gusted between the ridges and billowing clouds scudded across the sky. There were always other pilgrims within sight, all following the road upwards till a memorial cross was reached, where the way ahead became a track heading to a woodland path. It was here that they caught up with Eduardo, an earnest-looking young surgeon from Brazil, whom Wade had met the previous night at the Refuge Municipal in St-Jean. They stopped to rest and studied the memorial.

"I wonder how many people have died doing this walk?" said Wade. "At the refuge last night, some of the guys were talking about a man who fell to his death just a few days ago."

"I'm told it's about three a year on average," said Matt, "though that doesn't seem many considering the vast numbers of people who walk the Camino these days."

"I did the Camino a couple of years ago," said Eduardo. "It was in summer and there were far too many pilgrims. It shouldn't be so crowded now, at this time of year."

They continued to climb steadily, eventually passing the stone that marked the border with Spain. They had now reached the Spanish region of Navarra, with its capital city Pamplona just a couple of days' walk away.

"You know, I have a very special reason for doing the pilgrimage at this time," said Eduardo when they stopped for a rest. "I've come to give thanks for the birth of my baby daughter. She was born prematurely, after a very difficult pregnancy, but now my wife and daughter are both healthy and happy." He showed the others a photograph on his smartphone. "I miss my family already, but I have exactly a month to walk to Santiago before I have to return to Brazil."

"If you run short of time you can always take a bus some of the way," said Matt. "I've walked this route before, too, but when my knee plays me up, which it will, I won't hesitate to take a bus when necessary."

Eduardo shook his head. "No, that's not possible for me. I have to walk all the way and carry my own bag. That's my Camino. It's important for me to do it right. There was a guy at the refuge last night who wanted to reach Santiago in less than three weeks, but that's a race, not a pilgrimage."

They walked on through some scattered woods until they reached the highest point on the route at Col de Lepoeder. From here on, it was all downhill to Roncesvalles. But which way? There was a choice.

At the pilgrims' office in St-Jean, Wade had received a warning that the direct route, straight down the mountain through the beech forest, was slippery and could be dangerous at this time of year. The road route to the right was recommended, but it was much longer.

He looked around and what did he see? Across the road and falling steeply to the left was the signed way, a leafy path disappearing into the forest below. He felt he had walked more than enough for one day and wanted to get down the mountain as quickly as possible. So, diving down the steep path through the forest, where the fallen leaves lay knee thick on the uneven ground, he slid and stumbled towards Roncesvalles, their goal for the day, which lay somewhere at the bottom of the slopes. The others followed, but more cautiously.

Eduardo and Matt were soon some way behind, but even though Wade was descending rapidly another pilgrim caught up with him before Roncesvalles. It was a sturdy, middle-aged Korean man he had noticed at the refuge in St-Jean and also on the mountain. Actually, he hadn't noticed him so much as his girlfriend (at least Wade had assumed it was his girlfriend), a striking, dark-haired beauty with a lovely smile, at least twenty years younger than the Korean.

"Where's your girlfriend? You haven't left her on the mountain?"

The Korean looked puzzled for a moment, then smiled. "Oh, you mean the young Austrian girl. No, she's not my girlfriend. Her name's Maja and we met on the train to St-Jean. We walked together for a while, that's all. She's lovely but much too young for me." He paused, then added, "I wouldn't leave my girlfriend on the mountain."

The Korean told Wade to call him Lee. "Nobody in the west can pronounce my first name, so I just use my family name here."

They finally reached the abbey in Roncesvalles where the pilgrims' hostel, the Albergue de Roncesvalles, was located. By this time, mid-afternoon, having gone without a drink for most of the day, they were both very thirsty. Ahead to their right stood the imposing abbey and albergue, while to the left Wade noticed a bar and it seemed to be open.

"We can either check in at the albergue now and have a beer later," he said, "or we can have a beer now and check in afterwards."

Lee smiled. "Let's have two beers before we check in," he said.

The Albergue de Roncesvalles, which had been recently renovated, looked smart and new inside. A lot of pilgrims were already established in the long dormitory, which was divided into a line of cubicles, each with four bunks, two up and two down. Wade was pleased to be able to get a lower bunk, as he didn't relish climbing up the ladder. He looked around and soon found Eduardo, who had put on his glasses and was tending his blistered feet with a surgeon's care.

"Hi, Eduardo! Is Matt here too, or is he still struggling down the mountain?"

"No, he made it okay, but I think it was hard on his knees. He's here somewhere. We're going to eat the peregrino menu in the albergue tonight at seven. If you want to eat too, you must reserve a place."

"Thanks, I'll do that, but what's a peregrino?"

"Wade, you must learn this word now. Peregrino is the Spanish word for pilgrim. That's what we are – peregrinos."

*

That night, though the dormitory was quite full, it wasn't too noisy and it was certainly warm enough.

This was something of a relief because he had only packed a lightweight sleeping bag in order to save space in his backpack. The pilgrims' menu in the evening had been satisfying and he had slept well, but far too early the following morning the lights came on and religious music began to play over the loudspeaker system.

It again took an age to pack his things and he was beginning to wish he had got a slightly bigger backpack. He should have brought light shoes or sandals to wear in the evenings, so that he wouldn't have to wear his walking boots all the time, but he simply had not been able to find any room for them. In the end, out of sheer desperation, he had packed his bedroom slippers, which could be squashed flat and took up almost no space, and these were the last items to be squeezed into the top of the backpack. Finally, he was ready and despite being among the last to leave the albergue he was on the road by eight, but without any breakfast – just water from the kitchen. However, it was a beautiful morning, with the promise of a lovely sunny day ahead, and he walked briskly past the road sign announcing 790 kilometres to Santiago, eager to get on with the adventure.

In spite of his complaining muscles and sore feet, walking was much easier than the previous day when crossing the Pyrenees. There were few steep gradients and the scenery was pleasant and pastoral, with cows and sheep grazing lazily in the fields. A line from a poem came into his mind. What was it? Something like: 'God's in his heaven, all's right with the world.' But who wrote it? And what was the rest of it? He didn't remember, but he didn't care either. He just felt good inside.

Contrary to expectations (this being a Sunday) there were enough cafés and even a shop open in one of the pretty villages he walked through, so there was no problem finding something to eat for breakfast. For much of the day, he walked alone, at his own speed, taking a break when he felt like it and enjoying the solitude. Along the way he met up occasionally with other pilgrims, including Lee, Eduardo, an English couple with their small daughter enjoying a picnic at the wayside, three Spanish girls walking together and chatting continuously, and a young Hungarian eager to practice his few words of English.

Shortly before the last descent into Zubiri, which was his target for the day, he caught up with Eduardo again. It had just gone three o'clock when they walked across the old bridge into the village and checked in to the Zaldiko – a small private albergue. Who else should be there but Matt from Chicago, who had already showered, changed, and was resting on his bunk.

"Hi, you guys. Good to see you. There's a bar across the street so we could go for a beer later."

"Great!" said Wade. "A beer is just what I need, but I have to get cleaned up first. I've got some laundry that needs doing too."

"The hospitalera will do it for you for a few euros."

"Hospitalera?" Wade was puzzled. "Is that some kind of washing machine?"

The other two men laughed.

"That's another word you must learn for the Camino," said Eduardo. "The person who runs the albergue is called the hospitalero, if he's a man, or hospitalera for a woman."

Later on, in the bar across the street they met up with Nathan, a chubby, fresh-faced young Canadian Wade had seen on the mountain the day before. Nathan had already been walking for a few weeks, having started at Le Puy in France, and both Matt and Eduardo had walked the Camino de Santiago before, so Wade felt very much the novice of the party.

After just two days on the way, he sensed that the next stage to Pamplona could be a tough one. He had read somewhere that the third day of walking is when you hit the wall. How would it turn out for him?

*

The day started well enough and after an early breakfast they all set off together. Their route criss-crossed the Rio Arga for much of the way and on one quiet stretch of the tree-lined river, they saw the beautiful Austrian girl who had walked with Lee in the Pyrenees. Her backpack was lying on the ground and she was leaning back against a tree trunk on the river bank. Her eyes were closed, her arms outstretched and her hands open. She was facing towards the gentle autumn sun, meditating, apparently oblivious to the four men walking silently by.

"Wow!" said Wade in a whisper, after they had passed her. "What a stunning sight! I don't think I've ever seen a lovelier girl than her," he continued, more to himself than to the others.

"Yes," said Matt. "She is lovely. She's very religious too. I got to know her after the pilgrims' mass in Roncesvalles. She told me she meditates every day and wants to visit and photograph every church along the way to Santiago."

"That's a lot of churches," said Eduardo. "I think she'll find that many of them won't be open, so she'll have to be content with taking pictures from outside."

They walked on, and though this stage was not particularly long or demanding, Wade grew very tired and was relieved when they eventually reached Pamplona, world famous for the Festival of San Fermin and the running of the bulls. Of course, that would be in summer, when the city was full to overflowing with tourists from all over the world, but now, in late autumn, the place was quiet enough.

As they checked in at the Albergue Jesus y Maria, right in the centre of the old town near the cathedral, Wade noticed that he was somehow physically and mentally disoriented. He could not think straight, could not find his documents and then when he did find them he dropped them. This feeling of confusion and lack of coordination reminded him of the time, years before, when he had done a lot of running. It was a feeling he used to get at the end of an exhausting long-distance race. Later on, in a nearby bar, he mentioned this experience to the others.

"It's not unusual," said Matt. "The Camino is a bit like doing a half-marathon every day, carrying a heavy backpack. I was pretty groggy too. We're probably not drinking enough, so let's have another beer."

Eduardo was looking at his smartphone. "Great idea! Also some good news for me. My Spanish friend José will be joining me here in Pamplona and we will walk together to Santiago. I met him on my last

Camino two years ago and I've sent him a message to come to our albergue tonight."

That evening they had dinner at a small restaurant in the old town, where they were also joined by Maja. Matt had invited her when he saw her arriving at the albergue earlier and Wade wondered if he was taking more than a paternal interest in the girl. Who could blame him?

"Now we are becoming a real peregrino family," said Eduardo, "just like on my last Camino."

Wade looked at him, questioningly. "Peregrino family?"

"Yes, it's usual on the Camino. You see the same people nearly every day. You sleep at the same albergues, you eat your peregrino menus together in the same restaurants, you share with each other, you get like a family."

Back at the albergue, they met up with José in the foyer. He was middle-aged and not very tall, but he was sturdily built and looked fit. With his goatee beard, he reminded Wade of a sixteenth-century conquistador.

When they entered the dormitory, it was already quite full. The bunks were in blocks of four, located in cubicles which were open to the corridor on one side for access. Pilgrims of both sexes were getting ready for bed and when the lights went off, it was very dark. In spite of many people snoring, Wade was so tired that he quickly fell asleep.

Sometime in the middle of the night, he woke up. He needed to go to the toilet. He groped his way through the darkness, carefully passing by the many cubicles of snoring pilgrims until he came to the door at the end of the corridor which led to the toilet area. Afterwards, when he returned to the dormitory, he began to feel his way back up the corridor towards his bunk. But which cubicle was it in? He could see practically nothing in the gloom. Nervously he felt his way along until, by touch, he found the position where he thought his bunk should be. All was quiet and still and he carefully reached for his sleeping bag. Suddenly he froze, for under his hand was an arm, a slender arm with soft, smooth skin – the arm of a young woman. The figure in the sleeping bag stirred but didn't wake up and Wade gently withdrew his hand. Then, passing silently on to the next cubicle, he found his empty bunk at last and with a sigh of relief climbed into his sleeping bag. But he was disturbed by images that had been hiding in the back of his mind for so many years and it took ages before he could get to sleep again.

*

Wade's pilgrim family gathered in a café just around the corner from the albergue for a breakfast of coffee and a croissant. Nathan would be leaving them in Pamplona as he had a flight booked to Canada and there was no time for him to walk further.

"Are you flying back to Canada right away?" José asked him.

"No, not directly. I'm going to visit friends in Bilbao for a couple of days before flying back home." Nathan paused thoughtfully. "But I'll be back to finish my pilgrimage next year I hope."

José nodded. "Yes, a lot of peregrinos do the

Camino in stages. Not everyone can afford the time to walk it all in one go."

They said goodbye to Nathan and set off on the next phase of their journey towards Santiago. Wade reflected on how little they had actually seen of Pamplona, but they were pilgrims and not tourists and the arrowed way was all-important. Once the city had been cleared they had a steady climb up to the famous wrought iron pilgrim figures at Alto del Perdón. There were many wind turbines here, spinning and humming in the cool breeze that had sprung up. They paused to look back and admire the panorama of the Pyrenean mountains stretching to the horizon, while above their heads white, fluffy clouds scudded across the sky. After this, the stony ground fell for some kilometres until they got down to valley level again.

Wade walked alone for much of the time, meeting up occasionally at various resting places with Eduardo, who continued to suffer with his blistered feet. José, an experienced walker who had done many Caminos over the years, was usually ahead of them, while Matt was walking and viewing churches with Maja, some way behind.

The weather was unexpectedly sunny and warm for late October. Wade had learned his lesson from that thirsty first day in the Pyrenees and took care to make sure he always had fresh water to drink. Unlike the second day out, when, in his dehydrated state he had gone the whole day with just one stop to urinate, he was now back to normal. Or was he? For many years he had suffered from an enlarged prostate but had never taken the PSA test advised by the urologist when he was living in Germany. He had worried before the Camino that he would have to keep getting up at night to go to the toilet, but so far there had been no big problem. He might have to get up once a night, but so too did many of the other pilgrims at the albergues.

As he stood at the side of the track and urinated onto the grass, he remembered an article he had read by TV presenter Michael Parkinson, who had revealed that he had undergone an operation for prostate cancer. Looking down at the stream of urine landing well before him on the ground, he recalled one particular remark that Parkinson had made, to the effect that if you can hit a wall from a distance of two feet, then you've not got prostate cancer. For the first time in a couple of years, Wade could do this. He had thought till now he probably had cancer. It was perhaps a hidden reason for his doing the Camino at this time. It might be his last chance for such an adventure. While he didn't believe in rejuvenation or miracle cures, it did make him wonder a little. It was almost as if, in some mysterious way, he was getting younger.

They reached their destination for the day, Puente la Reina, a medieval town of great historic interest, where two routes, the Camino Francés and the Camino Aragonés, converged on their way to Santiago de Compostela. Here, the famous Romanesque bridge that gave the town its name, arching its way across the River Arga, marked for many the real start of their pilgrimage.

The weather had turned noticeably colder, with a touch of rain in the evening, and Wade was relieved to find a blanket for his bunk at their albergue to supplement his lightweight sleeping bag. He hoped that it would be enough. Otherwise, he was feeling in good shape again and twenty kilometres plus per day didn't seem quite so daunting any more.

In the evening he walked into the small town, with Eduardo and José, to find somewhere to have dinner. There were few places open this late in the year, but eventually they found a restaurant that advertised a pilgrims' menu. As they entered the small restaurant, Wade noticed the Korean girl he had first seen in the Pyrenees at Orisson. She was sitting at a table with another pilgrim, a slender, fair-haired woman in her early thirties.

"Why don't we sit together?" José suggested, and they moved another table over so they could all sit around it. "By the way, my name is José, next to me is Eduardo, and the young man with the white hair is Wade. Do you know, he told me he is sixty-nine years old and a grandfather. It's hard to believe."

They all sat down and ordered food and wine.

The Korean girl, who looked very young, was shy at first and introduced herself as Tina because she thought her Korean name might be too difficult for them.

"What do you do, Tina, when you're not on Camino?" Eduardo asked her.

"I was a student," she said. "I just graduated in the summer and now I'm travelling before I start a career."

The young, fair-haired woman, who sat directly opposite Wade, told them her name was Angelina and she was from Sweden. Wade was fascinated by her sparkling blue eyes, which seemed to look right into him.

"Where are you from, Wade?" she asked.

"I'm English," he said, "but I spent many years in Germany. In fact, I'm a genuine Opa – I have two German grandchildren."

"Hallo Opa!" she said, smiling mischievously. "What medication do you take to keep looking so young?"

"Oh the usual, you know, blood pressure pills, multivitamins and pumpkin capsules."

"Ah! Pumpkin, for the prostate."

Wade was rather surprised she knew what the pumpkin capsules were for.

Eduardo and José ordered more red wine and later they all drank some Spanish schnapps. There was much laughter and joking and they forgot about tiredness and aching limbs, so they didn't notice how time was passing. They walked back along the narrow cobbled street to their albergue and discovered, when they eventually arrived there, that it had been locked shut for the night and they had to hammer on a window to get someone to open up and let them in.

They chatted and joked for a while longer before turning in. Wade had a top bunk this time and climbing up the ladder with sore feet was not so easy. The bottom bunk was occupied by another newcomer to the party, a tall, athletic-looking man in his mid-forties – Simon from Oxford.

*

Wade was getting into a routine now, on this, the

fifth day of his pilgrimage. Packing his gear every morning was becoming an automatic process and no longer a big event. For breakfast, his family arranged to meet up at the first open bar that they came to, before continuing along the narrow, cobbled street leading the way through the quiet town to the ancient bridge, with its many arches, to begin the next stage to Estella.

Wade walked with Matt much of the time. The way led through open farmland and vineyards, interspersed with small villages, each with narrow streets, and stone houses nestling in the sunshine round an ancient church. They progressed steadily and in silence for a while, the only sound being the tapping of Matt's walking poles on the ground.

"I see you're a plodder, like me," said Matt after they had been going for an hour or more.

Wade nodded. "Yes, it's easier if I get into some sort of rhythm, and more conducive to thinking too. It gets so I don't always notice my surroundings, because my mind is off somewhere else. I'm trying to come to terms with my past and find a new direction for the remainder of my life."

"We all have our different reasons for doing the Camino," said Matt. "My first wife died of cancer a couple of years ago and it hit me hard. We had known each other since our college days and it was a match made in heaven. After her death, I was a broken man and that's when I did my first Camino – to seek help from God. Without the Lord and my church, I wouldn't have pulled through."

"And this time? Do you have a special reason this

time too?"

"Indeed I do." The big man looked across at Wade, his face shining with joy. "After a while, I got to know another woman, a widow, and our situation brought us ever closer together. We're members of the same church back home and now we've decided to get married. This new pilgrimage is a celebration and thanksgiving for my new life." He paused and smiled before adding: "It's also kind of addictive."

"What is? The Camino or getting married?"

Matt laughed. "The Camino, of course, though I must admit I do enjoy being married. I don't like living alone."

"But your future wife didn't want to come with you?"

"No, she's more of a city girl. She's not one for hiking or staying in hostels, but when I get to Santiago she'll be there to meet me and we will pray together in the cathedral."

He paused for a moment before asking: "Do you have faith in God?"

"I don't know what I believe in," Wade replied. "That's the problem. I'm getting old now and somewhere in the Bible it says that the years of man are threescore and ten – that's seventy years, so time is getting very short. It seems to me like this is the right moment to make this pilgrimage and to attempt to find my spiritual path before it's too late. When I was young, I was a believer, but somewhere along the way I lost it."

They walked on in silence and Wade thought back

to his early childhood, to the time of austerity in the years following the war, and his relationship to a strict father who had spent too long fighting Germans. Both his parents were religious, and as a small child, Wade had been taught to say his prayers every night before he went to sleep. Sometimes, if he had misbehaved during the day, his father would put him to bed and read a warning passage from the Bible. The Book of Revelations was a favourite, with its visions of hellfire and eternal damnation for unrepentant sinners, so from an early age, Wade had learned what it was to be ruled by the fear of God. As a result, he became a very 'good' child, determinedly avoiding doing anything that could be interpreted by his parents as being sinful. Later, at Sunday School, his belief had been reinforced by learning how, through Jesus Christ, he could reach the bliss of heaven by being 'mild, obedient, good as he'. Thus it was that he had become a Christian, without any doubts, until the end of his childhood.

Wade and Matt were among the first arrivals of the day at the municipal albergue in Estella, but by late afternoon most of the family had drifted in. Among them was Maja, who arrived with a dark-haired, good-looking man in his mid-thirties. After greeting Wade, she introduced her new friend.

"This is Danilo," said Maja. "We just met today. He's from Argentina."

For a moment, Wade was a little apprehensive – after all, relations between the UK and Argentina were not the best – but Danilo was open and friendly. As the three of them chatted together, Wade sensed the chemistry between Danilo and Maja and felt a pang of regret for the lost years since the break-up of his marriage.

That evening, Wade and a few others decided to have dinner in the town and they arranged to meet at the entrance to the albergue. When Maja arrived, she asked them to wait just a few minutes more because she had invited the newcomers, Simon and Danilo, to join them. Wade smiled to himself. He had a feeling that Maja's Camino would not be entirely about religion and photos of churches.

*

The following day they planned to walk to Los Arcos, a relatively short stage of just over twenty kilometres. Wade walked with Maja until they reached Irache, with its ancient monastery and Benedictine church. After trying the wine at the famous wine fountain, Maja went on to see if she could visit the church, while Wade continued by himself.

Like many of the pilgrims, he often preferred to walk by himself, while others travelled in small groups. He was a bit of a loner by nature, content to experience the solitude along the way, although he did enjoy having the company of his fellow pilgrims at the albergues.

It was a pleasant, relatively undemanding walk and he saw many pretty, orange-yellow butterflies that fluttered near the track in every patch of sunlight. He had never seen butterflies like this before, and so late in the year too.

Villamayor de Monjardín was his last chance for a break before the long, remote stretch through to Los Arcos, so he stopped briefly at the village bar for refreshment before walking on past vineyards and mixed farmland towards his goal. He began to drift into his subconscious self, plodding on monotonously, scarcely noticing his surroundings, asking himself the big questions. There was nobody else in sight, or at least he thought so, but just as he reached a junction, where another track met his, he was startled to find an elderly, grey-haired and bearded pilgrim walking next to him, staff in hand, looking rather like Gandalf in Lord of the Rings.

The stranger raised his hand in greeting. "Hola! I will I join you for a short time."

Wade smiled, a little warily, and greeted the old man briefly. After a few minutes silence, the stranger spoke again.

"My name is Diego. I am always on the Camino de Santiago and I talk to people on the way. This is your first Camino."

Wade wasn't sure if this was a question or a statement. "Right!" he said. "How do you know?"

"It's not so difficult. I observe and I am sensitive to the feelings of true pilgrims. I notice that you are reserved and self-controlled, but this is not really your nature. You are suppressing something."

Wade felt uneasy at the stranger's perception. "You could be right," he said cautiously, "but I'm not ready to let go yet."

There was silence for a few moments before Diego spoke again. "You are always seeing the same people on the Camino," he said. "We will surely meet again before Santiago, maybe several times. Buen Camino!"

Wade walked on as before, looking neither to left nor right at first, a little disturbed by what the weird old man had said to him. Then, when he finally turned round to look in the direction he had come from, there was nobody in sight. He shuddered slightly and a chill ran through his body. This was eerie. Was he losing control? Had he imagined this meeting?

He shrugged his shoulders, turned his face again towards the west and just walked for a while before the final descent into Los Arcos. Then, when he arrived at the main square of the small town, he saw Matt and Simon sitting at a table outside a bar. They were drinking cold beer in the sunshine and he just knew it was time to stop for the day. He pulled up a chair and joined them.

*

Early the following morning, Wade and his friends left their albergue in Los Arcos together and began the long stage to Logroño. It was All Saints Day and a public holiday in Spain. Once again the sky was clear and the temperature was pleasant for walking. Much of the route was off-road, along paths and tracks through the open countryside, but with a few steep sections to test the pilgrims. Then, shortly before Logroño, they entered the province of La Rioja, the home of Spain's most famous wines. There were vast vineyards on either side of the track, while on the northern horizon the rocky profile of the Cantabrian mountains dominated the scene, stretched out against the background of a clear blue sky. Though the harvest was over and the vines were bare, except for a few reddish autumn leaves that had yet to fall, some of them next to the track had been left untouched, with grapes hanging temptingly. Wade was curious to know why.

"This has been done deliberately," José told him. "It is a gift for the peregrinos."

They continued on their way, finally arriving at the lively city of Logroño where they soon found the municipal albergue. By late afternoon, Wade's complete pilgrim family had arrived.

"If you like," said José, "we could go together to the tapas bars this evening. I was in this city last year, and there is street nearby with many bars where we can have tapas and a drink and then move on to the next one."

"Nice idea," said Eduardo, "but we have to be back at the albergue by ten o'clock, or we'll be locked out."

"That's true, but maybe we can bring some tapas and wine back to the albergue and have a party in the kitchen. It's quite big. There is a table there and chairs too. What do you think?"

There was general agreement, at least among the younger members of the family, that this was a good plan of action.

"It's Simon's birthday today," said Maja, "and tomorrow he has to leave us and return to London. We can make it his birthday and farewell party."

When they went out in the evening, there was rain in the air. Nevertheless, Wade couldn't face the thought of putting on his walking boots again and so he went out in his bedroom slippers, much to the amusement of his companions. The tapas bars were very quiet so early in the evening.

"It's a pity that we have to go back at ten o'clock. That's when they start to get lively," said José. "Never mind! Eduardo and I have bought some good things to take back to the albergue with us."

They only managed to visit three bars before it was time to return to the albergue. By now, it had started raining and the streets were wet.

"The local people are staring in amazement at your footwear," said Angelina. "Slippers could become a trend here next year."

"Maybe I'll come back next year to find out," Wade replied. He nearly added 'if you'll come with me', but then thought better of it. He was fascinated by this young woman, but she was surely no more than half his age.

Back at the albergue, where another group of young pilgrims joined them in the large kitchen, the party was soon in full swing. Matt muttered something about this not being the purpose of his pilgrimage and went off to bed. Someone produced a bottle of strong alcohol, 'Licor de Orujo', to add to the wine and beer that was already available in quantity. A pilgrim with a guitar began to strum and they all sang 'Happy Birthday' to Simon, who was beginning to look a little glassy-eyed. He and Danilo were vying for Maja's attention, which she appeared to enjoy, while a dark-haired, middle-aged man was trying to get off with Angelina, who didn't seem very interested. Several of the male pilgrims were getting a little drunk.

Wade looked around him. He was the oldest of the partygoers by at least a generation and perhaps it was time to leave the young ones to it. He left the kitchen without speaking and went to his bunk in the dormitory, though not without some feelings of regret for his lost years – those years of living without a woman since the breakup of his marriage.

*

Wade and Matt said their goodbyes to Simon before setting out on the long, hard stretch to Nájera the next morning. They often found themselves walking next to the highway and there were many local walkers and bikers under way, taking advantage of the long weekend. The two men were alone at first but were joined later by Maja, while they were taking a break in a bar near the small town of Navarrete.

Wade always liked to keep some loose change available for stops like this. Village bars, with relatively few customers outside the main pilgrim season, were sometimes unable or unwilling to change large-denomination notes. So when Maja took out a fifty-euro note to pay for her small glass of orange juice, he expected some kind of reaction from the barman. But no – Maja knew how to use her charms. The look of innocence in those blue eyes and a winning smile were more than enough to seduce any barman into happily scraping together forty-nine euros change.

Maja told Wade and Matt that she had already taken over seven hundred pictures, principally of churches and cathedrals, but as they walked on after leaving the bar, Wade was interested to ask her about more secular matters.

"How did you enjoy last night's party? It was getting quite lively when I went to bed."

"It was nice," she said, "even though some of the men had too much to drink. I was a little sad, too, because it was Simon's last night with us. We discovered that we have a lot in common. We are both left-handed, we have the same star sign and we like the same music."

"Sounds like he might be the right man for you. It was obvious that he likes you."

"Yes, I like him too, but he's so much older than I am. You know, he's over forty and I think that's too old for me."

Maja stopped later to meditate, while Matt and Wade pressed on to Nájera, where they arrived in the late afternoon sunshine, after crossing the bridge over the Nájerilla River.

The municipal albergue, a single-storey, barrack-like building, was located near the river. The hospitalero, who was friendly and talkative, examined their passports as they checked in.

"Ah, Patrick!" he exclaimed, noting Wade's middle name on the registration form. "We have the same name. I am Patricio. This way please, you can choose any of the bunks on the left side only. The right side is closed for the winter."

The bunks were arranged closely, too closely, in a long row the whole length of the building.

"They're practically double beds," said Wade.

Matt looked along the row of bunks doubtfully. "Well, I guess I'll take my chance sleeping next to you, otherwise there's no knowing who I'll be sharing with. Let's take this lower pair here, near the door, so it's not such a long march in the middle of the night if I need the restroom."

Other pilgrims arrived, including the rest of their family, until nearly all the available bunks were taken. Angelina, who had arrived with Maja and Danilo, took the upper bunk next to Wade and Matt.

"I hope I'm safe with you," she said with a smile, "but there's a guy further down the row who tried to accost me at the party in Logroño and I don't want him sleeping next to me."

Wade wondered what Angelina would think if she could read his mind. She was lovely, but so young, and he certainly wasn't young anymore. A voice inside his head told him not to get carried away, but that night he dreamed of his pilgrim family and especially of her.

*

Wade and the others had become used to fine weather and the following day lived up to expectations. They had a relatively short stage ahead of them to the town of Santo Domingo de Calzada, with its historic cathedral, and their quiet route was mainly via broad tracks through gently rolling farmland.

Wade walked alone, wrapped in his thoughts, paying just enough attention to the changing landscape to ensure that he didn't miss any of the painted, yellow arrows or way-marks that showed his route. Otherwise, his mind was free to roam as he plodded on, walking rhythmically and whistling softly to himself. It occurred to him that he nearly always whistled when he was alone, just like all the other old men he saw back home, strolling alone in the park or going round the shelves in the supermarket. It was a generation thing. Only the old men did this – the young guys didn't whistle. He tried to stop it, but after a while, he noticed he was whistling again. He needed to work on this.

After stopping for a second breakfast at a bar in the small village of Azofra, he walked on, trying hard not to whistle. Some time later he noticed two distant figures sitting at the side of the track, resting and enjoying the sunshine. When he got nearer, he saw that the two figures were Angelina and Maja, and he had almost the feeling that they had been waiting for him. But of course, that was just wishful thinking on his part. Why would they wait for him? Perhaps they were expecting some of the younger guys to come along – Danilo maybe? Yes, that would account for it.

He drew ever nearer, and after greeting him Maja walked away from the track and onto the farmland behind. Wade thought that maybe she was going off to meditate, or perhaps she needed the toilet, so he didn't watch where she went. He stayed for a few minutes, standing on the track, talking to Angelina, before going on his way. That was all very odd. Was it his ever more fertile imagination, or had she really been waiting there for him? Had Maja disappeared just to give him the opportunity to talk to Angelina alone? It surely couldn't be, or had he missed the opportune moment and let his golden chance pass him by? Wade walked briskly on, trying to put such thoughts behind him.

He caught up with Matt shortly before reaching Santo Domingo, where they checked in at the municipal albergue. It was only two o'clock and there was plenty of time to drink a beer and do the laundry while waiting for the others to arrive. The albergue was a large one, but as only two of the dormitories were in use to accommodate the off-season pilgrims, both rooms were full. Wade made a mental note of the comfortable-looking sofas in the lounge area, adjacent to the dormitories. If the snoring in the night became too bad, he could try his luck in the lounge.

That evening, Wade's entire pilgrim family decided to go out together and have a meal at a restaurant in the town. But where? None of them was familiar with Santo Domingo, nobody had any fixed idea, and nobody wanted to dictate to the others what they should do – or so it seemed to Wade. They were joined in their search for the ideal restaurant by another pilgrim at the albergue – Erika, dark-haired and petite, an American journalist in her early forties who lived and worked in Paris.

They drifted through the streets, unable to find a likely venue with a table big enough to accommodate them all. Matt, who in any case liked to eat early, began to get frustrated. Eventually, he gave up on the others and marched off to eat alone. At last, the rest of the party found a restaurant that could provide a table for eight and though the meal was nothing special, it was enjoyable to be able to share it together as a group. The young Korean girl, Tina, was again one of the party.

"What's your real first name?" Wade asked her.

"Min-Joo," she said, "but nobody here knows how

to pronounce Korean names."

"I'll try," said Wade. "For me, you're Min-Joo from now on."

She smiled at him.

Back at the albergue, after a couple of beers, they all turned in for the night and then the fun began. Wade just couldn't sleep. Everyone around him seemed to be snoring and his feet were cold. Eventually, he got up, dragged his sleeping bag with him, and tried to sleep on a sofa in the adjacent lounge area. But he slept only fitfully and was already awake first thing in the morning when the early risers left the albergue to start their day's walk.

*

After a much-needed coffee and a pastry Wade set off towards Belorado. The morning sky was clear at first, but then little by little the dark clouds gathered and the wind increased. For a time he walked with Matt and Min-Joo, but mostly he trudged on alone, battling against a fierce wind and driving rain. There were no bars or cafés open in the villages he passed through, but in Viloria de la Rioja he decided to take a break anyway.

He found shelter from the rain and wind in the porch behind the village church, where he could sit down and eat the apple he had in his pocket. For a moment he thought he was alone, but then he saw a shadowy figure in the corner of the porch, staff in hand, watching him silently. It was Diego, the ancient, grey-haired pilgrim he had encountered just a few days before, on the way to Los Arcos.

"Today is not so easy for walking," said Diego.

"After the warm sunshine comes the cold wind and the rain. The weather can change suddenly on the Camino, just like life itself."

Wade nodded in agreement. "Yes, today's weather is certainly quite a contrast to yesterday."

"Change is inevitable," said the old man. "We must learn to live with it and accept it. We are born, we grow up, we become old, we die. There is no elixir of youth and we cannot turn back the clock. Any attempt to do so is an illusion and will cause us suffering."

"But there's no need to grow old before our time," Wade replied, feeling somewhat irritated by Diego's words. "Or do you think that at sixty-nine I should be waiting for the end in a care home?"

Diego smiled. "Of course not. But just be careful what you wish for."

Wade didn't reply, but after taking the apple from his pocket, he searched in his backpack for a knife to cut it into two pieces, so that he could share it. After rummaging for some seconds he found the knife, but when he turned around again the old man was no longer there. Wade shrugged his shoulders and ate the apple.

After some minutes, mulling over what Diego had said, he left his shelter and trudged onwards through the driving rain, and by the time he realised that he had left his knife lying in the church porch, he was halfway to Belorado. With head down, and teeth clenched tight, he pressed on, only to find that Belorado was closed, with not a soul to be seen in the empty streets. At least that was what he thought at first until he eventually stumbled on the only albergue that was open in November, situated near the main square of the town.

Matt was already there, sitting on his bunk, binding up his right knee which was giving him ever more problems, day by day.

"I'm going to have to take the bus to Burgos tomorrow and rest up a couple of days. I'll never make it otherwise. How're you doing?"

"Not too bad," said Wade, "only a few minor aches and pains."

There was only one dormitory available and gradually it filled up as their family and other pilgrims arrived. Later on, the albergue would offer a peregrino menu, but Wade and a few others, including Angelina, decided to go out to a small restaurant in the main square instead. In the event, they had a lively evening, with a lot of red wine and Orujo.

As they all raised their glasses before drinking the first bottle, Maja said urgently, "No, not like that! You must look in the other person's eyes when you touch glasses, otherwise it means nothing." She paused a moment. "If you don't look in their eyes, you will have seven years' bad sex."

Even though they all laughed, they took her message to heart and raised their glasses again, taking care to look each other in the eyes as they said, "Salud!" Even so, at the back of his mind Wade wondered if, at his age, seven years' bad sex would really be such a disaster.

*

The following morning, he was packing his gear ready for the day's march when he noticed his rain jacket was missing.

Angelina came over to him. "Lost something?"

"Yes, it's my rain jacket. I must have left it in the restaurant last night. It's not expensive but I don't really want to lose it, because the weather doesn't look so good any more. I'd better hang around until the restaurant opens and then try to catch you all up."

"Let me have your mobile number," said Angelina. "Then I can let you know where we've got to." Wade gave her the number and she sent him a text.

Ok, now you've got my number too. Good luck! See you later.

While the others set off on the next stage, Wade waited impatiently for the restaurant to open. It wasn't until shortly after ten that the girl who had been their waitress the previous evening arrived and unlocked the door. She recognised him right away and gave him his jacket, which had been kept behind the bar overnight.

After thanking the waitress and putting on his jacket, he sent a text to Angelina to tell her he was finally on his way. Some time later he received a reply.

Ok. Did you find the jacket? We're now in villafranca, first bar, called 'el pajero'.

He texted back right away.

Yes, I got the jacket. Just went through villambistia. Lesson for today: red wine bad for short term memory. Wade x

He checked his guidebook. He was five kilometres short of Villafranca, which would take him about an hour to walk. The others would almost certainly have left by the time he got there.

He pressed on, walking quickly, eyes on the path ahead, oblivious to the surrounding countryside. Then, as he approached Villafranca, he noticed a red-coated figure in the distance waiting for him at the side of the road. He could scarcely believe his eyes – it was Angelina and his heart nearly missed a beat when he saw her.

She greeted him with a smile and a wave. "Hi, you look like you've been hurrying."

"Yes, I've been trying to catch up."

"The others have only just left. We had a long second breakfast at the bar over there." She indicated the bar across the road. "I think you'd better take a break too before you go on. There's a steep hill to climb after Villafranca and no more bars or cafés until San Juan de Ortega – that's another thirteen kilometres."

"Yes, you're right. I think I'll take a short break here."

She smiled again, her blue eyes looking deep into his, showing concern. "Don't overdo it, okay? See you later."

Wade followed her advice and went into the bar for a second breakfast, but he didn't stay there long before setting out again up the steep hill that led out of Villafranca. He wanted so much to catch her up – this blonde-haired angel with the clear blue eyes and winning smile. As he walked on, two contradictory statements went continuously through his mind – 'Faint heart never won fair lady' and the downbeat

'There's no fool like an old fool.' At sixty-nine, he was at least twice her age. Just because she liked him as a friend didn't mean that she saw him as a potential lover.

"Don't get carried away and spoil the friendship," he muttered to himself. "Don't be an old fool."

The old adage reminded Wade of his childhood Sundays and he smiled at the recollection of that time. The Sabbath had always been spent with the family, which included the morning service at the local church, where Wade was in the choir, then going to his grandparents' for Sunday lunch and afterwards listening to the 'Billy Cotton Band Show' on the wireless. Billy Cotton himself was a lively old man, full of gentle humour and fun, but every Sunday, without fail, Wade's grandfather would make the comment: 'There's no fool like an old fool.' The young Wade had thought this a strange thing to say and had never forgotten it.

Once he had climbed the first hill, the track broadened out with woodland to either side, but Wade hardly noticed his surroundings, he was so engrossed in his thoughts. After a time he came to a stone monument, a memorial to those who had fallen during the Spanish civil war. It was covered in many newly laid wreaths of flowers, and he stopped there for a few quiet moments before marching quickly on again along the track through the pinewood.

At last, he saw her in the distance. She was sitting in the sunshine with Maja, on a grassy bank next to the track. He wasn't going to walk on by again. This time he was sure they were waiting for him.

The three of them sat a while longer on their grassy bank, enjoying the sunshine and sharing some chocolate. When they eventually moved on, Maja dropped behind, deliberately it seemed, so that Wade and Angelina could be alone together.

They walked together all the way to San Juan de Ortega, talking about their lives and interests, though on reflection Wade felt that it was much more about his life than hers. She had a direct way of asking pertinent questions and he told her about Tamsin, the first real love in his life; about Sabina, the girl he married; about his years in Germany and his final return to the UK. It was like being questioned by an angel in a beautiful dream. Wade felt his heart racing. He was not normally as open as this. Was he finally falling in love again, after decades of smothered feelings?

Of course, there were some things he could not tell her; things he never talked about to anyone; things he hardly ever even thought about. They were his guilty secrets, tucked away at the back of his mind as if they had never happened. Only Diego, in some strange way, seemed to know that he was suppressing something.

"Do you have a special reason for your Camino?" Angelina asked him.

"Yes, I suppose I do," he answered cautiously. "I feel it is time to take stock of my life, look ahead at my plans for the future and above all try to find my spiritual way." He paused. "And what about you?"

"When my long-term relationship came to an end, just a few months ago, it was a hard time. I felt lost without a partner. Then, finally, I decided I needed to build my life again, see if I can do things on my own."

"But why the Camino in particular?"

"I love Spain. In fact, I spent much of my childhood here, because my father was working for an international agency based in Madrid."

"So that's why you speak such fluent Spanish. Would you like to live here again?"

"Maybe, but I'm settled in Stockholm now, my family and friends are there and I like my work."

Wade was thoughtful for a few moments. "You know, José told me that in his opinion most people who walk the Camino have either come to the end of a relationship or they've lost their job."

Angelina laughed. "He could be right, but in any case, it's difficult to find time to do the complete Camino de Santiago in one visit if you have a job. That's why I have to stop when we get to Burgos and fly home. I have to go back to work next week."

Wade was silent for the moment. This news was a hammer blow to his emerging hopes.

"When is your flight?"

"On Friday afternoon. We should arrive in Burgos on Wednesday, so I'll have a full day there before going home."

"I'll be sorry to see you go," said Wade. But deep inside he meant much more than that. 'Sorry' was inadequate to express what he felt at that moment.

The albergue at San Juan de Ortega was closed for the winter, so after a short rest they walked on a further few kilometres to Agés and checked in at the albergue there. Most of the usual suspects turned up eventually, and that evening they enjoyed a great paella and a beer before retiring.

As so often, there was little space between the bunk beds in the dormitory, but this time Wade didn't mind. His bunk was right next to Angelina, within touching distance in fact. He noticed that she wore a mask to cover her eyes.

"I can't sleep unless it's very dark," she told him.

In the event, nobody slept too well except for a middle-aged French lady who was snoring loudly in the opposite corner of the crowded dormitory. Wade was lying on his back with his eyes open, and in the gloom he saw a hand reaching out from the next bunk. It was Angelina. She found his shoulder and shook it, while he gently placed his free hand on hers. Angelina sat up with a start. "Oh, I'm sorry. I thought it was you who was snoring and I wanted to wake you up," she whispered as she withdrew her hand.

There was no way he could sleep after that. He lay awake for hours, his mind whirling with thoughts of the girl in the next bunk. What was happening to him? In his mind he began to compose a short poem to her, about their meeting on the Camino, walking together, then saying goodbye in Burgos and wishing he were much younger. He hoped he would remember it in the morning so he could write it down. He hadn't written a love poem since he first met his ex-wife, all those years before.

3. BURGOS

In the morning, after breakfast, Wade noticed that Maja left the albergue alone with a glint of tears in her eyes. Danilo, looking dispirited, watched her leave.

"Anything wrong?" Wade asked.

Danilo shrugged his shoulders. "We've split up… at least for the moment."

"I'm sorry to hear it. She's a very lovely girl."

Danilo looked at him directly. "I know this, of course. That's what makes it so hard. But we both want to do our own Camino and it's not possible when we are together."

While Maja and Danilo went their separate ways, the rest of the group stayed together for much of the time after leaving the albergue, subconsciously realising that this would be their last day as a pilgrim family before it became fragmented once they got to Burgos.

As they climbed the misty slopes of the Sierra Atapuerca, Wade told Angelina of his conversation with Danilo that morning.

"I will be sorry if they really break up. I feel they belong together."

Angelina laughed. "You're too romantic. You know, I've talked to them both many times and I'm sure it's just a holiday flirt. Nothing has happened."

"I think it goes much deeper than that," said Wade. "Anyway, what can happen when we all sleep together in one dormitory?"

When they reached the large wooden cross at the highest point of the Sierra Atapuerca, José pointed ahead through the morning mist, which was just beginning to rise.

"We will soon be able to see Burgos in the distance. But don't be fooled, it's further away than it looks."

They stopped a few minutes to rest and to take some photos at the simple cross, all except Eduardo, who plodded steadily on, his feet at last free from the blisters that had plagued him in the first days. José told them that he and Eduardo were planning to press on with their Camino after spending just one night in the city, though they proposed having a break from the usual albergue.

"We will take a small hotel for one night near the city centre," said José. "Why don't you join us? If we share rooms it will not be too expensive and we don't have to be back by ten o'clock in the evening, like in the albergue."

Wade, Erika and Angelina agreed this was a good idea, but Min-Joo decided she would stay at the albergue near the cathedral in Burgos with the Korean boys.

As they grew closer to the city, Angelina said she would like to walk the last few kilometres of her short Camino alone, so the others went on ahead. The approach to Burgos was along a busy road which ran next to the perimeter fence of the airport.

"Quite a contrast to what we've been enjoying till now," said Wade.

"Yes indeed," said José. "But Wade, please walk at the side of the road now, not in the middle of it. I don't want to pick you up in pieces."

As they approached the outskirts of Burgos, they reached the stop for the city buses. José proposed that they wait for a bus.

"It's only concrete, factories and traffic from now on until you get to the city centre. It's not good for walking. By bus, we will be there in a few minutes."

"Great idea," Erika agreed. "Let's just wait a minute for Angelina. I can see her coming right now."

"But I am going to walk," said Min-Joo. "I want to walk every step of the way, with no buses."

Wade smiled at her. "That's my Camino too."

"Okay," said José. "You can walk, but we'll take the bus and find a hotel. Wade, send us a text when you get to the cathedral square and I'll pick you up to take you to our hotel."

Wade and Min-Joo left the others at the bus stop and when they finally neared the old city they caught

48

up first with Eduardo and shortly afterwards with Maja – two more who intended to walk every step of the way. While Eduardo and Wade waited for José in front of the cathedral, the two young women went on to the albergue, which was situated nearby. Maja planned to stop an extra day in Burgos, but Min-Joo wasn't sure yet. Wade gave her a big hug before she left, just in case they missed each other on the way.

José had found rooms for them at the Hotel Norte y Londres, situated in the old city and only a few minutes' walk from the cathedral. The three men would share one room, while Angelina and Erika shared another. Compared to the albergues they had all grown used to over the past twelve days, it was a real luxury.

This would be their last evening together as a group. José and Eduardo wanted to start the next stage of their Camino the following morning, while Erika had to catch a train back to Paris. Of the party, only Wade and Angelina were staying in Burgos another day.

Wade plucked up the courage to suggest to Angelina that they could share a room at the hotel the following night. Why not? They had been sharing rooms in the albergues for long enough.

"No, I'd like my own bathroom for a change," said Angelina. "There's a hotel just down the road where single rooms are a little cheaper."

*

The following morning, the three men left the Hotel Norte y Londres and went into the bar on the other side of the street for a last breakfast together before they travelled their separate ways. After a time Erika came in to join them, but there was no Angelina.

"It'll have to be a quick breakfast for me," said Erika. "My train leaves in just over an hour and I don't know where the station is yet."

"Where's Angelina?" Wade asked.

"She's still in the room," said Erika. "She's decided to stay there another night, rather than change her hotel."

Wade had felt a premonition that she might do this, but he was disappointed, nevertheless. Obviously, she wanted to keep him at a distance. He, himself, would be staying at the cheaper hotel further down the street, but with a whole day ahead in Burgos there would be a chance to spend some time with her again. He would send her a text later.

After saying goodbye to his Camino friends, Wade took some time to relax back at his hotel, where he could write postcards and send emails to friends and family.

An email that he sent to one of his German friends gave him particular satisfaction. Wade remembered their conversation a month or so before, during his last visit to Frankfurt, when they had met at a pub for a few beers and a schnitzel and he had announced his intention to walk the Camino de Santiago.

"What! All that way, at your age! I give it two weeks before you give up. You mark my words. I won't say anything more about it, but you'll be back within two weeks for sure."

But though the two weeks were up now, he was feeling fit, strong and eager to walk all the way.

He was about to exit from his email account when he noticed a new message in the spam folder. It was from the solicitor who had acted for him when he sold his mother's house in north London, and not spam at all. He had intended to just take a quick look before deleting it but changed his mind when he read it.

He skimmed through the message again until he found the passage that interested him.

...we received an enquiry from an American lady (Eve Dawson) who is trying to contact you about a 'family matter'. She traced you as far as your former address and found out from the current owners that our firm had acted for you in the transaction. We don't release confidential information about a client without express permission, but we did agree to pass on her email address to you, for you to contact her if you wish (see below). Ms Dawson asked us to mention the name 'Amy' but gave no further information about...

He was unsure what to do. The name, Eve Dawson, meant nothing to him, but to get news of Amy after all these years, decades even, brought back recollections of an episode he had mentally removed from his life. And now? He did not want anything to get in the way of his Camino experience, but all the same, he transferred the email to his inbox. He would keep it for the present and deal with it at a later date.

His emails finished, Wade went out to explore. He also wanted to buy a cheap pair of plastic sandals to replace the tatty slippers he had been wearing every evening at the end of a day's walk. Above all, he wanted to visit the famous Gothic cathedral that dominated the old city of Burgos.

Wade had just a short walk from his hotel, through the bustling streets of the old town, to reach the open square in front of the towering cathedral. He had been feeling quite emotional all morning with the knowledge that this first part of his pilgrimage had come to an end and he had said goodbye to Camino friends he would probably never see again, though he would always remember them fondly. In addition, he was disturbed by long-forgotten passions that had been suppressed for so many years.

He climbed the short flight of stone steps up to the main entrance of the vast cathedral where, once inside, he was moved by its majesty and aura of holiness. All around him were elaborate gilded images, carvings and sculptures, while high above the main nave a magnificent vaulted dome dominated the scene. It was awe-inspiring.

There were few visitors at this time to disturb the peace and he walked softly forward up the long nave towards the high altar. He was filled with emotion. It was years since he had entered a church, let alone a majestic cathedral like this. If there was a God, he could surely be found here. Wade entered a pew towards the front, away from any tourists, and knelt down. With tears trickling down his face, he began to pray quietly but fervently.

"Oh God, if there is a God, whoever you are, whatever you are, I just want to thank you for getting me this far on my Camino. Thank you for the wonderful people I have met. Thank you for making me feel young again. Thank you for Angelina, and please let me see her again if only to say goodbye." He paused, unable and unwilling to stop his tears, before adding, "If she left without saying goodbye it would break my heart... again."

A few minutes passed before he managed to compose himself sufficiently to stand up and leave the cathedral. What was happening to him? He sat down on a bench in the square, where he took the mobile phone from his pocket and texted a message.

Hi Angelina, i guess you know i moved to the other hotel. It's ok. When can i see you today? Don't leave without saying goodbye. Wade x

He was so engrossed in what he was doing that at first, he didn't notice the other figure sitting on the bench.

"Hola," said the grey-haired old man sitting next to him. It was Diego. "I didn't want to speak until you were ready. It's a beautiful cathedral, isn't it?"

"It is indeed," said Wade softly. "I felt very moved."

"I can see that in your face. Burgos is a pivotal moment on the journey to Santiago. You can divide the Camino into three stages – body, mind and spirit – and the road to Burgos is the first of those stages. Until now it has been a kind of adventure holiday, enjoying the exercise, getting fit, meeting new people." He paused for a moment before adding, "Maybe finding romance?"

"What are you implying?" Wade replied, somewhat sharply.

"I'm sorry if I offended you," said the old man, "but for some people, sex becomes the sole object of their Camino and they turn aside from the spiritual path they had intended to follow. The decision is yours of course, but be aware of the dangers."

Before Wade could think of a suitable reply, Diego had vanished.

Looking back, it occurred to Wade that his belief in God had vanished at about the same time as his interest in sex had appeared. There had been no place for religion in Wade's teenage years. His thoughts had been concentrated on girls and sport and he had felt that he would live forever.

He remembered his first sexual experience with Barbara – a 'quicky' on the school playing field, behind the cricket pavilion. He was just seventeen years old then and a sixth former, while she was a couple of forms below, so she couldn't have been more than fifteen. Even so, Barbara was the one with experience and had a reputation among the lads of being an easy lay. In the event, it certainly was a 'quicky' and was over almost before it had started.

On his way back to the hotel, Wade was reflecting on what the old man had said when, suddenly, he heard the mobile phone buzzing in his jacket pocket. It was a text message from Angelina.

I'm going to meet danilo and maja at 8. If you want I can pick you up at your hotel? Otherwise some beers at 10? x

He smiled, kissed the screen of his phone and texted back.

Pick me up at 8. It will be good to see the others too. Wade x

He was waiting in the foyer of his hotel when Angelina arrived. They walked on to the 'Casa Pancho', a popular pinchos bar in the old city, where Danilo and Maja were waiting for them. Wade was glad to see his two young friends together again, even though they planned to go their separate ways the following day.

"I want to spend a day more here in Burgos," said Maja, "while Danilo wants to move on tomorrow. We will meet up again later."

Shortly before ten o'clock, Danilo and Maja had to leave in order to get back to their albergue before it closed its doors for the night. Wade and Angelina stayed on, sitting close together on high stools at the long bar-counter, while the place became ever more crowded with new arrivals from the street. Despite it being busy and noisy in the bar, the atmosphere was relaxed and Wade felt the intimacy of his nearness to Angelina, their bodies almost touching, They ordered more red wine and pinchos and Angelina started, quite casually, to ask him about personal relationships – a theme they had begun when walking together on the way to Burgos.

"When your first partner left you and went to America, how long were you alone?"

Wade was silent for a few moments. He thought of Amy, then pushed the thought back into the hidden recesses of his mind where it belonged.

"It must have been a couple of years, I suppose. I had put my job on hold in order to spend a summer travelling in Europe, and it was towards the end of this trip that I met my future wife.

"Where did you meet her?"

"In Greece. It was very romantic. We only knew each other for a few days before she returned to Germany and I had to go back to London. A couple of months later she came to visit me and er… well, she just stayed and stayed. We lived together in London for two years before moving to Frankfurt."

"I think you told me before that your wife, or should I say, ex-wife, is twelve years younger than you?"

"That's right."

"How old was she when you stopped having sex together?"

"I'm not sure any more. Maybe about thirty-six."

"And you've not had sex with a woman since then?"

Wade felt the questions were really getting too personal now. He shook his head in disbelief.

"Nobody's ever asked me such intimate details of my life before."

"I'm very direct," she answered with a smile. "It has to do with my work I expect."

"Didn't you tell me you work in Human Resources?"

"That's right, and I have to interview a lot of job applicants."

"And what kind of questions do you ask them?"

"I usually end up asking them about their sex life."

They both laughed and after some initial hesitation, Wade continued.

"The end of my marriage hurt me more than I could bear, so I closed my heart to any new relationship. I've been... how should I say it... celibate ever since then."

Angelina looked thoughtful for a moment.

"So you've never had sex with a woman older than thirty-six? That's why you're not looking for a woman of, say, fifty or sixty now."

This came as something of a revelation to Wade. But it was true. He had never moved on.

"If you've not been with a woman for so many years, what do you do for sex?"

Wade shook his head in disbelief.

"I masturbate," he said simply.

"How often?"

"Ugh! What a question! Maybe a couple of times a week."

"Do you watch porn?"

"Rarely, I normally use my imagination."

They were silent for a few moments, and then Wade spoke again.

"What about you?" he said. "You told me before that you and your partner were together for several years, but you split up a few months ago. What do you do for sex now?"

Angelina blushed slightly. "If I ask such questions I have to expect this I guess. I masturbate too, of course." She paused and then went on: "What about on Camino? Do you do it in the showers?"

He laughed. "No. After walking twenty-five kilometres a day I'm usually too knackered for sex."

"It may be a good idea to buy some Viagra."

"You think I need it?"

"It's nothing to be ashamed of. I know men in their forties who take Viagra."

"Like your ex-partner?"

"Well, yes."

"Then he was much older than you, too."

She laughed. "Older men seem to like me for some reason. Did you know you're not the only one to take an interest in me on the Camino?"

"You mean the guy in the albergue at Logroño?

"No, not the one who accosted me at the party. I think he was just a bit drunk."

"Who then?"

"José. He was also interested, but I turned him down too. He told me he was forty years old, but he looks more than that, no?"

"Nearer fifty, I'd say."

Angelina looked thoughtfully into her glass, gently swirling around the last drops of wine in it.

Their glasses were empty again. Wade, with his few words of Spanish, just about managed to order more wine and some snacks. While one of the bartenders poured the wine, another brought them the pinchos. They spoke to each other in Spanish and then Angelina joined in. The man who had brought the pinchos looked embarrassed, but Angelina laughed.

"What was all that about?" Wade asked her.

"The guy who brought the pinchos said, 'These are for the young lovers.' He didn't realise I speak fluent Spanish too."

For a second, Wade didn't get the irony. He had forgotten that he wasn't as young as he felt in his heart.

They sat in silence for a while, eating and sipping their wine, before Angelina continued.

"It's fine that you want a woman again. You are a good-looking guy and you will find someone to love if you look for a woman who is nearer your own age."

"That's all very well, but you're the one I've fallen for. It's just that it's taken me such a long time to find you."

"I know, Wade. But you must be realistic." She smiled, looked at his hair and stroked it. "I like younger men with black hair. What colour was yours before it turned grey?"

"Darkish brown I think. I'm not even sure anymore, but I would dye it black for you."

She laughed. "I don't think so, Wade. You're okay with grey hair. Just find yourself an older woman."

The bar didn't close until two o'clock in the morning and they were the last customers to leave. They walked side by side along the empty, silent street until they came to the Plaza de Alonso Martinez...

"Here's my hotel," said Angelina softly. "This is where we must say goodbye."

They embraced in the middle of the deserted

square, and as he kissed her gently on the cheek he felt her mouth turning towards his. When their lips touched, she pulled and sucked tenderly on his bottom lip, sending a tingle of pleasure down his spine, and whenever she paused he reciprocated, pulling gently, slowly, on her top lip. Their embrace tightened. Wade had not experienced such an erotic kiss for many years. He felt the start of an erection.

She backed off a little, though still in his arms, and smiled up at him. He nuzzled against her upturned forehead, not wanting this moment ever to end.

"I must go," she whispered finally. Then, after one last kiss on his cheek, she turned around and walked quickly into the hotel without looking back.

4. MIND

After a sleepless night in his lonely hotel room, Wade sent Angelina a text while he was having breakfast.

Thanks for the therapy. It was wonderful to get to know you. Keep in touch. Wade x

He would have liked to say so much more, but he was afraid of scaring her off. What would she want with love letters from an old man?

Leaving the hotel shortly after seven he walked through the old city, across the square in front of the cathedral one last time, and up the steps to join the route of the Camino again near the Church of San Nikolas. He walked briskly, automatically registering the yellow arrows marking the way, but otherwise noticing little. He could think only of Angelina, the intimate conversation in the Casa Pancho and, above all, that final kiss in front of her hotel.

What did it all mean? Why had she kissed him like

that? His head was whirling. The evening's revelations and that kiss at the end had rekindled memories of long ago.

He remembered Tamsin, the first great love in his life, the mysterious, dark-haired beauty he had got to know at university in London. It had all been rather wonderful at first, sharing a shoddy bedsit in Putney and enjoying the carefree student life. But ten years later, when Tamsin had become ever increasingly involved with a New Age spiritual society, with headquarters in the USA, their relationship had foundered.

Wade grimly recalled that fateful night when she told him that she was committing her life to the sect in America. They had just finished dinner and it was clear she was steeling herself to make an unpleasant announcement.

"I really am going to California," she said suddenly. "I want to be where we are strongest."

She paused for a moment, looking hard at Wade, before continuing.

"I'm not coming back, Wade. I'm going there for good." Then another pause. "Do you think there is any way we can continue our relationship?"

Only by giving his soul to this crackpot sect could he have kept her. After a long silence, his mind in a turmoil of anguish, he finally spoke those last bitter words: "No. I never want to see you or hear from you ever again."

But he had missed Tamsin badly and had gone to pieces for quite a while after she left, at least emotionally. At that time he had been teaching maths at a co-educational grammar school in West London and it had been a struggle to keep on top of his job, but at least it had taken his mind off the loneliness of his private life. Then, one day he had met Amy and…

He jerked his mind back to the present. He had never told anyone about Amy. He had airbrushed the episode from his life, though it was something he would never get over completely. He had managed to find a comfortable place to put it, hidden away at the back of his mind, but it was always there. Would it come back to haunt him?

There were very few pilgrims on the way as he left Burgos, but shortly after passing through the outskirts of the city he caught up with a tiny Japanese lady with a big smile, and a mop of black hair that seemed to bounce on her head as she walked. Her name was Ayumi and she was probably in her mid-fifties. They chatted briefly before Wade marched on ahead. He needed to be alone with his thoughts.

Some time later he saw a figure coming towards him. It was a stocky, middle-aged man who, from his clothing and backpack, looked like he must be a pilgrim too. But why was he walking the wrong way? As they drew nearer, the stranger stopped and spoke.

"Hola, are you from Germany?"

"No, I'm English, but I can speak German."

"It's all right, I can speak English too."

The man took some pieces of mangled plastic from his pocket and flourished them briefly before returning them to his pocket.

"That was my German debit card," he said. "I

tried to get some money at an ATM in the next town and it chewed up my card. I don't know what I'm going to do now. The only cash I've got is this." He pulled a few coins out of his pocket and showed them to Wade.

"Burgos is a big city, there may be a German consulate there that can help you."

"No, there's nothing," said the stranger. "I need to get to Madrid to find a consulate."

"You could phone your bank. They must have a number for emergencies."

"They can't help me either with a problem like this."

Having lived most of his life in big cities, where small-time con men abound, Wade's gut instinct warned him that the stranger was some kind of confidence trickster.

"Sorry, I can't help you," he said and walked on without looking back. Even so, he was just a shade uneasy in his conscience. What if the story had been genuine after all and he had refused to be a good Samaritan?

Some minutes later he heard someone calling him from behind. It was the Japanese lady he had met earlier and she came hurrying towards him.

"Hola," she said. "Did a man ask you for money just now?"

"Yes, in a way, though he didn't ask directly. Did you give him anything? If so, I hope it wasn't much."

She nodded. "Yes, but I only gave him ten euros. Do you think it was a trick?"

"I'm pretty sure it was," said Wade.

They walked together until the village of Rabé de las Calzados, where Ayumi stopped for a break and Wade went on alone once more. It suited his mood. Climbing up to the high, empty plains of the Meseta, he was blind to the landscape, thinking only of Angelina and wondering if he would ever see her again. He descended into the ancient village of Hornillos de Camino before making the gentle climb back up to the Meseta, following the dirt track which seemed to stretch endlessly before him across the lonely plateau. There were vast, dark clouds drifting across the wide sky and he was facing into a stiff breeze as he plodded on, head down into the wind, trying in vain to control his emotions. He felt lost and alone, in a state of limbo, every few minutes bursting into tears for no apparent reason.

His solitude was suddenly interrupted by a buzzing sound coming from his pocket. It was his mobile phone signalling an incoming text message. He stopped and took off his backpack before reading the message. It was from Angelina.

On the bus to the airport. End of this beautiful parallel universe called camino... I take nice memories, experiences and wonderful people home. Keep me posted about your camino or other love. Love yourself, open up your heart, you deserve it. Don't keep thinking you don't need it. Big hug for my special opa x

Wade gently kissed the screen of his phone and whispered, "Thank you, thank you…" over and over again. He had seldom felt so moved as at this moment and he made no effort to stem the flood of tears that streamed down his cheeks.

After some minutes he donned his backpack again and stumbled onwards across the Meseta. It had been a long day and he was tired, physically and emotionally. Hontanas, his goal for the day, lay just a few kilometres ahead, but he could see no sign of it yet, just the empty wilderness that surrounded him, until suddenly the track dipped sharply and the tiny village came into view at last.

At the albergue in Hontanas, the attractive girl in reception actually carried his backpack up to the dormitory for him. After finding his bunk and trying in vain to send Angelina a text, he was able eventually to send an email from the albergue.

Hi Angelina

I got your text message when I was on the Meseta, 25 km after Burgos. I cried many tears. I am now at an albergue in Hontanas, at the bottom of a deep valley, where I can't get a signal on my mobile. I went back up the hill, but I couldn't get a signal there either, so I'm now trying my luck with the internet at the albergue. I've walked very fast today and thought of you pretty well the whole time, occasionally bursting into tears and feeling very emotional. What's happening to me? I miss you very much.

With love

Opa Wade x

*

The following morning Wade was awake early – too early! A large group of eager French pilgrims in his dormitory had got up, somewhat noisily in the pitch dark, and departed long before he dragged himself out of bed. Why did they do it? Why were they in such a hurry?

After coffee and a croissant, Wade set out with the intention of walking to Frómista – a distance of more than thirty kilometres. The track was close to the road for much of the way to Castrojeriz and there was little shade, but it was a joy to feel the late autumn sunshine on his face. Was it still autumn? He supposed it was, though he couldn't be sure of the exact date any more. He would have to check that on his mobile phone.

Shortly after Castrojeriz, where there was a stiff climb up to the Meseta again, he noticed three men walking together some way ahead of him. As he drew nearer, it became clear that they were much older than most of the pilgrims he had encountered. In fact, they looked about his own age except, of course, that in his mind he didn't consider himself that old anymore. When they reached the rest area at the top, where the trio stopped to admire the wonderful panoramic view, he joined them.

The three men were all Spanish, old friends who had been walking from Burgos together, and one of them spoke fluent English, having lived for some years in Manchester.

"We are all nearly seventy years old now and have known each other since we were boys," he told Wade. "Last year we walked from Roncesvalles to Burgos, this year we are walking from Burgos to León, and next year, God willing, we will complete our Camino to Santiago de Compostela."

Wade was moved by the aura of peace and

fellowship that surrounded them. These men appeared at ease with themselves and each other, acceptance of the stage in life that they had reached, living for the moment without regrets and with faith in their God. He was envious of their serenity.

Leaving the three friends at the rest area, Wade continued on his way, descending from the Meseta to Itero de la Vega, a small village where he stopped at a bar for lunch. He ate a bocadillo and drank a beer, feeling more relaxed and less fraught with emotion than he had been the day before. Then he walked on along the track through open farmland until he came to a bridge over a small canal, where he noticed small, printed leaflets on the parapet of the bridge, weighed down by stones to prevent them blowing away in the wind.

Out of curiosity he took one and saw that it was advertising an albergue in Boadilla del Camino, which was the next village. He decided on the spot that Boadilla would be far enough for the day and went straight to the albergue 'El Camino' when he got there.

The dormitory was in a converted barn, with a cosy lounge area adjacent to it, and. after taking a shower Wade went out to look at the village. There was nobody around and no bars or shops open either. Then, as he was walking back to the albergue, who should he see but Danilo, wandering somewhat forlornly along the empty street.

"Hola Danilo!"

"Wade! You are staying here? Is the albergue okay?"

"Sure. Come and see for yourself. It's just around the corner."

As they walked back to the albergue, Wade asked about Maja.

"We've split up again and decided to do separate Caminos." Danilo shrugged his shoulders, then smiled. "But maybe we'll meet again later on."

There were just seven pilgrims for dinner at the albergue that evening and the food was good, particularly the homemade pumpkin soup. Before retiring early, Wade and Danilo agreed to set off together the next morning.

*

The walk to Carrión de Los Condes was 'a piece of cake', as the pilgrims tended to call any stage up to a distance of about twenty-five kilometres and without steep hills. The marked way, which followed the main road for much of the time, was rather monotonous and Wade was glad to have someone to talk to. He asked again about Maja.

"It was hard for us to separate," said Danilo. "She is a beautiful girl, but very young."

"I think you are right for each other."

"I don't know… maybe. In many ways, we are very different. I am thirty-six and a musician; she is twenty-four and works in a tax office. We don't have many interests in common."

"But you will see her again?"

"Yes, I expect so. We keep in contact." He was silent for a few moments, then added: "And what about you? You told me you like Angelina."

"Yes, very much. I think she's lovely, but I'm more than twice her age – that's the problem. It's an impossible relationship. She says I'm much too old for her, and she's right of course, but from my point of view she's not too young for me."

Danilo grinned. "You have the spirit of a young man, Wade. In any case, you don't look as old as your years. You have plenty of time to find a woman who is not too young for you. I will help you look for someone."

They both laughed, but Wade wondered if his friend's offer might be serious.

Although it was Sunday, they were lucky enough to find a village with a bar open where they stopped for a second breakfast. The bar was filled with men from the village, noisily enjoying their Sunday morning drinks, while presumably, their wives were at home or in the church, because there were no women present.

The two pilgrims ordered bocadillos and coffee, which they took outside to a small table in the sunny street.

Wade checked the date on his mobile phone. "November 10th already, but the weather is being kind to us," he said, removing his jacket. He was thoughtful for a moment, remembering something. "Last night was the anniversary of Kristallnacht."

Danilo looked at him strangely. "How do you know that? Are you Jewish too?"

"What? You are Jewish? I didn't realise." Wade hesitated a moment before continuing. "I lived in Germany for nearly thirty years and Kristallnacht is still remembered by people who care." He paused before adding, "Also, I had a Jewish grandmother."

"Maybe enough for the gas chamber many years ago," said Danilo quietly.

"I know."

"Are you religious, Wade?"

"I was brought up as a Christian, but I lost my faith. That's one reason for my Camino – to find my faith in God again. And you?"

"My real pilgrimage will start after the Camino," said Danilo. "Then I will go to Jerusalem, for a seminar on Jewish music, before I return home to Buenos Aires."

With breakfast finished, they continued their way towards Villalcázar de Sirga, each wrapped in his own thoughts. Finally, Wade spoke.

"You know I never felt Jewish at all until I went to live in Frankfurt. Then it kind of hit me, especially when I learned more about the Holocaust, and I started getting these nightmares."

"Nightmares?"

"Yes – bad dreams. I used to dream I was a Jew in the ghetto, on the run from the Gestapo. Wherever I fled they pursued me and no matter how hard I ran they would get nearer and nearer all the time, without ever seeming to hurry. Wherever I tried to hide, they found me. Then, in the end, I would get a knife in the back and wake up in a cold sweat. It was the same dream every time."

"But you stayed?"

"Yes, my wife didn't want to leave. Frankfurt was her home… and then the children came along."

"Ah, I understand. And you still feel bad about Germany, or no?"

"No, not anymore. Over the years I got used to living in Frankfurt and made some good friends there, but I always felt that somehow I didn't quite belong. For better or worse I knew I had to return home one day. It was an instinct, you know, like old elephants have."

Wade wondered why he had never told Sabina about his nightmares. She had asked him often enough when he called out in the middle of the night, but he had always pretended he could remember nothing. Why? He should have been more open about his feelings, instead of concealing them, but he had been afraid of losing her.

Upon reaching the main square of the village, they saw a fine church on one side and a busy, noisy bar on the other. They entered the bar, which was full of action. There were many people from the village enjoying a drink after church, and there were a number of pilgrims too.

"Hola Wade! Hola Danilo!" came a voice from behind them. They turned around and saw Min-Joo with Chu-Young sitting at a table near the door. They were greeted enthusiastically by the two young Koreans with a big hug.

Looking towards the bar, Wade noticed an attractive woman, with long fair hair and a beautiful smile, looking in their direction. She was one of a small group of pilgrims standing at the bar, drinking beer.

"Have you seen the woman with the smile?" said Danilo. "She's looking at you."

"More likely to be you," said Wade. But inside his head, he did wonder if the smile had been for him.

After a couple of beers, they walked the last few kilometres along the gravel track to Carrión de los Condes, where they soon found the albergue Santa Maria – a convent hostel run by nuns.

The dormitory was different to all the other albergues that Wade had stayed at so far, in that it had normal beds with fancy coverlets instead of the now familiar two-tier bunks. He had expected a convent hostel to segregate the sexes, but to his surprise, this wasn't the case. Looking around the large room, he recognised a few faces. All four of the young Koreans had now arrived, as had the woman with the smile together with her pilgrim family.

Wade's main priority, after showering and getting changed into fresh clothes, was to use the internet facilities at the albergue where he checked his incoming emails and then wrote one to Angelina.

Hi Angelina

Arrived today in Carrion de los Condes. The Camino is quite different since Burgos, much more introspective. For the first two days, I walked mostly alone – I wanted it that way to digest my 'therapy' and be emotional. But today I walked with Danilo and met up again with the Korean group, including Min-Joo, along the way. We're all staying at the same albergue and tomorrow we intend to walk to Terradillos de los Templarios, which is the halfway point between St-Jean and Santiago. Wish you were here to do it with us. When we were in Burgos, before that last evening together, I was moved to write a few lines of verse. They are for you.

The Camino's where I met her
And I never will forget her
For my heart stood still.
She was young and she was pretty
And we walked to Burgos city
As true pilgrims will.
But I'm too old to be her lover
And our time is nearly over
So I feel the pain.
Yet no matter how it hurts now
When I think about it, somehow,
I'd do it all again.

With love
Wade x
PS: I'd love to hear from you

Later that evening Wade and Danilo went out for dinner. They were dining at a small restaurant not far from the albergue, sitting near a window facing onto the street, when suddenly the door burst open and a group of pilgrims strolled in. Among them was the woman with the smile who, as the group passed by their table, made a point of greeting Wade and his companion with a friendly, "Hola!"

"I think she likes you," said Danilo.

*

The following morning Wade sensed that Danilo wanted some time alone and he set out with Min-Joo.

"I spent the last two days with Chu-Young," she told him. "But I think he misses the other Korean guys, so I decided to let him go this morning."

"That's lucky for me," said Wade with a smile.

The path to Calzadilla de la Cueza was along an old Roman road, the Via Aquitana, lined with trees for some of the way and running straight across the empty plains. There was very little shade.

"Your English has improved a lot since I first met you," said Wade.

"I was very shy at first and afraid to speak. It would have been easy for me to stay with the Korean boys, but that's not why I'm here. I want to meet people from other lands and make new friends."

"You're a good ambassador for your country."

"Thank you, I try to be. You know it's good that so many peregrinos can speak English, but I would like to learn some Spanish for my next Camino."

"Me too," said Wade. "I feel a little stupid sometimes when I can't understand what people are saying to me."

While they took a short break at a picnic area, the Korean boys caught up with them, arriving with a middle-aged man from the USA.

"And what part of Korea are you from?" the American asked Wade, jokingly.

Wade felt slightly irritated by the newcomer.

"I'm from London and this is my Korean

granddaughter," he answered with a straight face.

The American looked at him quizzically, not knowing quite what to believe.

Some minutes later, when Wade and his new granddaughter continued on their way, Min-Joo asked him, "Do you really have a granddaughter?"

He laughed. "No, but I have a daughter."

"How old is she?"

"Twenty-eight."

"That's only a few years older than me. I thought she would be nearer forty maybe."

"I was a late starter," he replied. "However, I also have a son and two small grandsons."

"But no granddaughters?"

"No, not yet anyway."

"Would you like one?"

"Yes, of course."

"Then I will be your granddaughter," said Min-Joo with a smile. "And you are my English grandpa."

"Agreed."

Notwithstanding it was mid-November, the sun was surprisingly warm and they soon drank most of their water supplies, so they were pleased when at last they reached a settlement that had a bar, with tables and chairs outside in the sunshine. Several pilgrims were already enjoying cold drinks and Wade and Min-Joo joined them. Soon the Korean boys and Danilo also arrived. Nobody walked by without stopping for refreshment, and having stopped, they were reluctant to leave.

Eventually, Wade and Min-Joo went on together, leaving their friends relaxing at the bar.

"I told the Korean boys we are going to the albergue in Terradillos de Templarius," said Min-Joo. "We will see them there."

After Caldadilla, as the two friends approached Ledigos, the last village before their goal for the day, Wade noticed that a large, scruffy-looking black dog just ahead of them kept stopping and looking back as if to check that they were following.

"This is a bit like taking the dog for a walk," he said.

They walked through the village of Ledigos without stopping, following the dog as if mesmerised, even passing an albergue and a lively bar without giving it more than just a passing glance. The dog led them on, always waiting for them to catch up before continuing, leading them towards their goal in Terradillos de Templarius just a few kilometres ahead. It was uncanny. Somehow Wade began to get an uneasy feeling, remembering the devil dog he had read about in Paolo Coelho's book. They weren't taking the dog for a walk – but was it taking them for a ride?

When they reached Terradillos, it was late afternoon. They were both tired, having already walked more than thirty kilometres that day, and they were looking forward to finally arriving at the albergue. The dog led them straight there and then sat down near the door, to which a notice had been pinned that read, 'Cerrado 11 Nov'.

"Shit!" said Wade with some feeling. "Today is the 11th. The place is closed, though it's supposed to be open all the year round. It looks like we should have stopped at the albergue in Ledigos."

He looked around at the street and noticed that the dog had disappeared. "The devil in disguise," he muttered to himself.

An elderly woman came towards them in the otherwise deserted street. "Mañana," she said, pointing to the albergue as she went by.

"Mañana too late," he replied somewhat bitterly.

In the meantime, Min-Joo had been busy with her smartphone. "I told the Korean boys that the albergue is closed," she said. "But they're almost here, so they decided not to turn back."

They set off to walk on to Moratinos, the next village, where there was also a small albergue, though they held no great hopes of it being open in mid-November. If the worst came to the worst, they would have to continue to Sahagún, but they didn't want to contemplate that possibility just yet.

They trudged into Moratinos and, of course, the albergue was closed for the winter, just as they had feared. While they were resting briefly, before taking the way to the next village, a large Mercedes car drew up beside them and a middle-aged lady lowered the driver's window and spoke to them in good English.

"I'm afraid all the albergues are closed until you get to Sahagún," she said. "That's quite a long way to go and it's getting late. I can give you a ride to the station in Sahagún if you like."

The offer was tempting, very tempting, but the two pilgrims were determined to walk every step of the way, without compromise.

"Thanks for your kind offer," Wade said. "But we are pilgrims. We have to walk."

When they reached St Nicolás del Real Camino, they stopped in the quiet village square for a few minutes to rest. The place seemed deserted. There was not a soul to be seen anywhere. Min-Joo took the last apple from her backpack.

"Wade, would you like this apple?"

"No, you eat it. It's your apple. But thanks anyway."

"We can share it. Have you got a knife?"

Wade shook his head. "No, I'm afraid I lost my knife. But I can try to break the apple in half if you like."

As he was trying in vain to break the apple into two pieces, a window in the house directly behind them opened suddenly, and a hand reached out and placed a pocket knife on the window sill. An elderly couple, who were sitting at the window, smiled and looked down on them. Wade cut the apple in half and, after wiping the blade, returned the knife to the window sill.

"Muchas gracias," he said, and the elderly couple smiled and nodded in return before closing the window again.

The two pilgrims moved on shortly afterwards. The sun was low on the horizon now and it was growing darker and colder. Min-Joo was listening to music on her smartphone and she gave Wade one of the earpieces so he could share the music too. It occurred to him, not for the first time, that sharing and helping were an integral part of the Camino.

After some time they stopped listening to music and began to chat. Min-Joo talked about her childhood and growing up in Seoul. Wade noticed how many of her remarks were prefaced with the phrase, 'When I was young…' For him, being young was any age up to his mid-forties, whereas for Min-Joo it meant her childhood.

"When I was young, I really wanted to be a boy," she said.

"Why was that?"

"Because everything I wanted to do, my mother would say, 'That's not anything for girls.' I was sometimes very unhappy."

"And now?"

"It's okay. Now I can usually do what I want, but the family is very strong in Korea."

A text message came through on her phone. She read it and grinned. "It's from the Korean boys," she said. "They asked me what I've found to talk to you about all day."

"Are you going to tell them?"

"No, I don't think so."

They left the narrow track they had been following and came to a major highway, where their path ran right next to the road. It was quite dark now and the lights of Sahagún were just visible in the distance. Occasionally, cars and trucks with dazzling headlights sped noisily by on the adjacent carriageway. Suddenly, Wade picked up the sound of voices approaching them from behind. It was a group of pilgrims who had been at the albergue the previous evening, and Danilo was with them. After the initial greetings, they all moved on together, with Wade next to Danilo on the narrow path.

"Some people at the bar in Ledigos told me they saw you go by," said Danilo. "I decided to follow, although they told me that no more albergues are open until Sahagún."

"We could have saved ourselves a long walk if we'd stopped there," said Wade.

"Never mind. I have some news you may find interesting. Some people in this group know the woman with the smile. She's not with them here because she's staying an extra day in Carrión de los Condes, to care for the many blisters on her feet. I can tell you her name is Gabriella, she is forty-two years old, and she comes from Italy. Maybe you will meet her."

The group trudged silently on along the dark path, then through the industrial area of Sahagún until at last, they reached the old town. The municipal albegue was hard to find and very basic. With Wade's group and the Korean boys, who turned up a little later, it was completely full.

The new arrivals went together to a nearby restaurant for dinner. Maybe it was because he had just walked more than forty kilometres and felt very tired, but Wade didn't particularly enjoy the company of this new family of pilgrims. Luckily, his friends Min-Joo and Danilo were also there.

He found two of the new pilgrims somewhat

irritating. Carlos, originally from Columbia but resident in the USA, was a man in his late forties with a smooth smile – almost certainly a man for the ladies. The other man was a few years younger, Philippe from Switzerland, tall, athletic and haughty looking. Wade had previously seen them accompanying the woman with the smile.

As soon as they returned to the albergue, Wade retired to his bunk. He wasn't feeling at all well, and it wasn't just because of the strenuous day he had experienced.

*

During the night he started to shiver, his head began to ache, and then he had to rush to the toilet because of a sudden attack of diarrhoea. In the morning, it was clear that he was too ill to walk very far.

"There is a private albergue in the next village," said Danilo. "I'll take you there and see if you can stay for a day or so until you get well again."

They found the albergue, which lay just off the Camino route in the village of Bercianos del Real Camino. When they arrived, Wade was more than relieved to take off his backpack and rest.

The albergue was run by a friendly middle-aged couple who didn't speak any English, so Danilo explained the situation to them in Spanish. After a short discussion, he turned to Wade.

"It's okay, amigo. You can stay here. The hospitaleros told me there have been a number of pilgrims lately with stomach problems, probably caused by drinking infected water. One guy had to go to hospital. But we are lucky, these people are very kind and will put you in a room by yourself."

"Muchas gracias," said Wade and smiled weakly.

"I will go now," said Danilo. "I want to reach León in two days and wait there for Maja. She sent me a message that she will look for me in León. Then we will be together again."

"I'm so glad you are going to see her again. Don't forget to keep in touch and tell me how you are getting on. Maybe I can catch you up later."

"Of course, we will keep in contact. Adiós Wade."

"Adiós amigo."

A few minutes after Danilo had left, who should arrive but Min-Joo and the Korean boys. "We met Danilo and he told us you are here," said Min-Joo. "We hope you get well again very soon."

She took a small leather keepsake from her pocket and gave it to Wade. "I want to give you this token of friendship," she said and gave him a big hug. "I will miss you, Grandpa."

Wade felt tears coming again. "I will miss you too, Granddaughter."

After his friends had gone he rested on his bunk in a small room at the end of the albergue where, for the moment at least, he was alone. He got up later and tried to eat something, but vomited shortly after. He also had acute diarrhoea. Would this be the end of his pilgrimage?

In the late afternoon, he heard the sound of new arrivals in the next room. Some time later the door opened and one of them came in, together with the hospitalera.

"Hola!" he said. "My name is Raul. The hospitalera told me about you. I will give you some tablets to help against the sickness. You must rest another day and drink plenty of mineral water, for the salts. Don't try to eat today. Maybe tomorrow evening, if you're feeling better, you can eat a little plain rice, okay?"

"But can I stay here tomorrow night?"

Raul conversed in Spanish briefly with the hospitalera before answering. "Of course. It's not a problem."

When they left the room, Wade opened a can of mineral water that they had given him and swallowed a tablet. He lay back on his bunk and in due course fell into an uneasy sleep.

*

Somehow he got through the night without vomiting again, though he was still suffering from diarrhoea, and by the time he got up the next day the other pilgrims had already left. Wade didn't feel great, but at least he felt he was over the worst.

He rested up most of the morning, enjoying the sunshine in the yard in front of the albergue and drinking green tea. Later on, he strolled as far as the village shop and bought some more cans of Aquarius mineral water and some salty snacks. By this time his laundry had been done by the hospitalera and he was able to hang it out to dry on the clothesline in the yard. At midday, he felt well enough to eat a little plain rice and he even contemplated moving on in the afternoon but thought better of it. His stomach was a little tender.

During the afternoon, the albergue began to fill up

and as evening drew near the late arrivals started drifting in. Wade was sitting in the kitchen when he saw the woman with the smile walking by the window. She wasn't very tall, with a youthful figure, and her flowing hair framed a young face. How old had Danilo said she was? Forty-two? She certainly looked younger. She saw him too, at least he thought so, though she pretended not to. His heart nearly missed a beat.

After checking in, she came to see him in the kitchen.

"Hola," she said. "I didn't expect to see a familiar face here. I'm so slow, because of my blisters. The hospitalera tells me you've been sick."

"Yes, but I'm feeling much better now. By the way, I'm Wade."

"And I'm Gabriella," she said. "Is your young friend here too?"

"You mean Danilo? No, he's gone on ahead. He wants to meet his girlfriend in León."

In the gathering darkness outside, they saw a shadowy figure passing by the window.

"That'll be my Italian friend Marina," said Gabriella. "I sent her a text to say I am here."

Marina came into the kitchen and greeted Gabriella in a flurry of rapid Italian. Like her friend, she was not very tall but had black curly hair and a fuller figure than Gabriella. She was also a few years older.

Later that evening, all the pilgrims sat together around the kitchen table for dinner. "Wade, aren't you going to eat anything?" said Gabriella.

"It all looks very tasty, but I'm staying on my boiled rice diet tonight. I want to be well enough to walk tomorrow. Then I'll eat normally again." Wade paused a moment before adding, "Er… would you mind if I walk with you and Marina tomorrow? I would like some company."

"No problem, as long as you don't want to leave too early in the morning. We tend to be slow starters."

Wade felt pleased with himself. He had made the contact, and later that evening he sent a text to Danilo.

Hi Danilo, still at the albergue clara, but will leave tomorrow. Guess what. The woman with the smile is here too. :) Wade

Almost straight away he received a reply:

Gabriella is there!?? Wow!!! It is your time for action!! Be careful! I have some info for you! She is very open-minded. You will like her!!! Be well for tomorrow but don't push yourself!!! OK!? Looking to see you soon! Bye

Wade wondered how Danilo always knew so much about the women on the Camino. And what exactly did he mean by 'she is very open-minded?'

*

Everyone loved the Albergue Clara. The hospitaleros were kind and generous and even provided a fine breakfast before the pilgrims set off on the next stage of their journey, though Wade was unable to eat much. He and his two new friends were the last to leave. He waited for them in the yard while they attended to their various leg pains and blisters.

Finally, they were ready and the three of them strolled gently on along the quiet road to the next village, El Burgo Ranero, where they stopped at a bar for a second breakfast. Wade, with his stomach feeling a little delicate, drank only a tea. He noticed that he hadn't yet recovered his full strength after his illness and was glad to rest for a while. He was curious to find out a bit more about his companions, particularly Gabriella.

"You seem to be something of a linguist," said Wade. "Quite apart from English and Italian, I've heard you speaking Spanish like a native too. I'm impressed."

"Thank you. Languages are my hobby and they're useful in my work too."

"What kind of work do you do?"

"For the past few years I've been working for an international organisation in Brussels, associated with the EU, but now I think it's time to make a change."

"You've quit your job?"

"Well, for now I've taken a sabbatical," Gabriella told him, "and I'm going to spend a year just travelling. Spain is my first port of call."

"And after Spain?"

"Jerusalem next, and after that... I don't know yet."

Wade recalled his own sabbatical, though they had called it 'dropping out' in those days. It was after he had lost his job, following the affair with Amy. Had Gabriella put her job on hold, or had she been pushed, like him? He quickly put the matter back into the hidden corner of his subconscious where it belonged.

Their path on to Reliegos was straight and flat, running alongside a quiet road, with only an occasional car to disturb the stillness. Yet again the sun was shining out of a clear blue sky, though there was a little shade where trees lined the way. After some time, when they stopped to rest on a bench facing the road, a car drove by and its occupants waved to them. They waved back.

"I know!" said Gabriella, with a grin. "Let's give the Mexican wave to all the cars as they go by."

Like children at play, they did this for a while, until eventually, a car stopped just ahead of them to see if they wanted to hitch a ride. "No gracias," they called out, indicating that they were just having a bit of fun.

A little later, when the women stopped yet again to tend to their blisters and leg pains, Wade walked on ahead to the village of Reliegos. There he found a bar, with tables outside in the sun at the side of the street. He ordered a beer, waiting for the others to arrive, trying to get his thoughts in order. Gabriella was attractive, she was vivacious and fun to be with. He took out his notebook and composed a short verse about her:

It was on the Meseta
I walked for a while
Next the girl with the smile
And those mischievous eyes.

The three pilgrims eventually reached the municipal albergue in Mansilla de las Mulas just before dark. The pace had been much slower than Wade was used to, but it served to remind him that the Camino wasn't a race.

It was here they met up with Richard and Julie, a Canadian couple Gabriella had got to know when she was in Burgos. Both were in their late fifties, but whereas Richard was tall, well-built and had plenty to say, Julie was small, slender and more reserved. They all shared a bottle of Burgos wine that Richard had brought with him, to celebrate the reunion with Gabriella, and later, after getting cleaned up, the five of them went out for dinner in the town. Wade ate cautiously, not wanting to risk further stomach trouble.

On their return, he wanted to quickly take advantage of the internet facilities at the albergue, He went online and checked his emails. There was one from Angelina, sent the previous day.

Dear Wade

I've just spent my first few days back at work and it was really nice to see my colleagues again. Sounds a bit strange I know, but they're also my friends. When I arrived home late on Friday, I was just in time for the big family reunion we have every year at this time. There was much good food and wine. I regained all the kilos I lost during the Camino ;)

It's been a while since someone last wrote me a poem, many thanks! Very cute and an interesting rhyme scheme too. You should write more!

Sounds like it could be true, what they say about body, mind and spirit... What made you feel so emotional about our conversation that last evening in Burgos and the text message I sent on my way to the airport?

I guess you'll probably arrive in León today? Is that right? I keep following your route on the map.

Wade, please don't make me the theme of your Camino - I guess there are other things you should be thinking about , and not me. But perhaps your outburst of emotion will help you find what your needs are, no?

Big hug

Angelina x

He replied right away.

Hi Angelina

Thanks for writing. I'll reply at greater length when I get to León (we should arrive sometime tomorrow). Your questions cannot be answered in a few minutes before lights out at the albergue. I've been a bit sick, so had to take a couple of days off Camino, but now I seem better. Quite a few peregrinos have had this stomach bug I believe.

Looking forward to León and then the third stage of the Camino, but I may have to buy some more clothes. The forecast is for colder weather. Danilo is in León right now and maybe Maja too, but perhaps you know that already.

I'll write again when I get the chance. Wish I had an iPhone.

With love

Wade x

He was sharing a room at the albergue with Gabriella, Marina and a young Spanish woman, and when he returned there, the others were already in bed.

There were the usual problems with his sleeping arrangements. He had only a lightweight summer quality sleeping bag, inside which he used a liner to give him much needed extra warmth. He had found from experience that he needed to first get into the liner and then (with some difficulty) ease his way into the outer sleeping bag. Tonight was no exception and it took him a minute or so to complete the operation.

Gabriella and Marina had bunks on the opposite side of the small room, but Wade was near the door and directly adjacent to the light switch and power point.

"Wade, could you please just switch off the light?" Gabriella asked sweetly.

"And could you please unplug my phone and the charger?" said Marina.

With a sigh, he dragged himself out of bed to do this and then had to go through the whole operation of getting into the two layers of sleeping bags again. From the other side of the room came the sound of muffled giggles.

He was almost asleep when he heard the faint buzzing noise of his phone under the pillow. It was a message from Angelina:

Take care of yourself and write me more when you have the chance. X

5. LEÓN

With Richard and Julie joining them, they left the albergue as a group of five pilgrims the next morning and ambled slowly along. They had a relatively short stage ahead of them, and the way to León was mainly on roads or paths running close to the motorway. Though there was nothing of great interest to look at, it was an enjoyable walk with lots of chat and several breaks for drinks and tapas.

The weather remained fine, but there was an icy cold wind blowing as they made their way through the dismal, industrial outskirts of León.

"Don't you feel the cold, Richard?" said Wade to the big Canadian, who was wearing shorts.

"Well, it can get pretty cold where I live, but I guess I'll be putting long pants on tomorrow."

They eventually reached the old town, stopping briefly to take photos in front of the magnificent

Gothic cathedral before going on to look for rooms at the nearby students' halls of residence, where they wanted to stay for two nights. The receptionist on duty spoke little English and so Gabriella, as the only Spanish speaker in the party, conducted negotiations.

"Okay, this is what we can do," she said after a short discussion with the receptionist. "Richard and Julie can have a double room here for two nights, the rest of us can have single rooms for tonight in another building nearby. The only problem is that for the second night only two single rooms are free, so one of us will have to move to a shared room in the main building for the second night."

Wade thought he had better do the gentlemanly thing. "I'll move out for the second night."

Gabriella looked hard at him. "Why?" she asked a little sharply.

"Well, as a man I thought…"

"It's no problem," said Marina. "I'll move out."

On their way through the narrow streets to the apartment building where their rooms were situated, Wade thought hard about Gabriella's reaction. Did this mean she wanted him to be near to her?

The accommodation was on an upper floor and once they entered the apartment they were in a combined kitchen and living room area. Leading from this was a corridor, with the bedrooms off to one side. Wade's room was next to Gabriella's, then there was a bathroom, then two further bedrooms (one of which was Marina's) and another bathroom. Wade hadn't seen such luxury since Burgos.

Wow! He had a single room next to Gabriella. Was he reading too much into this? It was all her doing, or so it seemed. He was feeling quite nervous. He found Gabriella very attractive and perhaps she fancied him too? Stranger things could happen, or at least he thought so. If it came to sex, maybe with Viagra he could perform even when walking twenty-five kilometres a day – but without it? Was she just being friendly to an old guy, or did she want good sex? He doubted if he was up to it, but it was beginning to look as though he might find out that night.

As he lay on the sofa in the living room, pondering these matters, Gabriella and Marina, having showered and freshened up, were now ready to depart for pilgrims' mass in a chapel near the cathedral.

"I'll call you when it's finished," said Gabriella. "We'll only be gone a little more than an hour, then we can meet up for dinner."

Alone in the apartment, Wade's thoughts turned once more to Angelina. She was the one he wanted really, but that seemed impossible. She had told him as much. Was it love he wanted from Gabriella, or was it simply a matter of sex after all those years without a woman?

The apartment was very quiet and he fell asleep on the sofa. When he woke up he noticed that it was already half past eight. He sent Gabriella a text:

That was a long mass. Am at apartment waiting to hear from you.

A few minutes later he received a reply.

In a bar with philippe and carlos. Pick you up downstairs in 5 mins.

Philippe and Carlos? Weren't they the two guys from the dinner party in Sahagún, after the day of the long march? This could be bad news for him. He went downstairs and waited outside the front door.

Gabriella arrived with Carlos and it was clear that she had already had a few drinks. Her face was flushed and she was very animated.

"The mass started later than we'd thought," she said. "Then on the way back we ran into Carlos and Philippe and went to a bar for a drink. We've not been there long."

When they arrived at the small bar, it was empty of customers except for Philippe and Marina. Wade felt uncomfortable. He was obviously intruding on an established foursome. Clearly, Marina and Carlos knew each other well, and Philippe rarely took his eyes off Gabriella who, bubbly as ever, was enjoying the attention.

Shortly afterwards, they all left the bar and walked on a few streets to a restaurant, where the group had arranged to meet up with Richard and Julie. At the table, Philippe took care to ensure that he sat close to Gabriella, while Wade was relegated to a seat at the opposite end. He was sulking, feeling angry with Philippe and angry with Gabriella. It was a strange feeling and one that he hadn't experienced like this for many years. Basically, he was jealous – but why? It was almost like being a teenager again, faced with the strains and frustrations of competing with another boy for the attention of an attractive girl.

With the meal over, they went on to a disco at 'Molly Mallone's', an Irish pub not far from the main square. It was crowded and loud, as discos are, and Wade wondered how many decades had passed since he last visited such a place. Of course, most of the people present were local and young, dressed up and out to impress the opposite sex; but it seemed like this place was also popular with the passing pilgrims because there was a fair sprinkling of familiar faces that he had met along the way. Most of the pilgrims at the disco were young too, but they could be easily distinguished from the local people by the clothes they were wearing. There was no room in a pilgrim's backpack for finery.

Wade and the others found some space near the tiny dance floor. He looked about him and saw that he must be easily the oldest person present. It was impossible to hold any sort of conversation, so he gave up that idea and just drank beer and moved to the music. They were obviously used to older pilgrims here because much of the music was from the seventies. In particular, there was a live act – a big guy in a shiny blue suit, with an Elvis quiff, who sang the hits of Tom Jones. Not bad, thought Wade, who had by this hour of the night consumed enough alcohol to loosen up and almost enjoy himself at last.

He danced alone, he danced with Marina, he even danced with Gabriella when he got the chance. Philippe, for his part, stood mainly at the bar, his eyes following Gabriella wherever she went. Now and then he would try to intercept her, but she remained elusive. Towards the end of the proceedings, when the DJ put on some slower, more romantic music, Philippe made his move and took her in his arms. Wade, who was looking on with some envy at first, noticed that Gabriella kept Philippe at a distance and when he tried to put his hands on her hips to draw her towards him, she pulled away. Wade, in his slightly befuddled state, found this interesting. Maybe there was hope for him yet.

In the small hours of the morning, the disco crowd began to thin out a little. In particular, the pilgrims, most of whom had a long day's walk behind them or were faced with another long walk after a short sleep, began to leave after fondly embracing all those who they had met along the way and wishing one another a slightly slurred, "Buen Camino."

Gabriella beckoned to Wade from the other side of the small dance area.

"Come with me please," she said and led Wade to the entrance door. "Wait for me here. I'll only be a minute."

Then she was gone and Wade waited, feeling somewhat bemused. What did this mean? What was going on?

She returned a couple of minutes later, with Richard, Julie and Marina. "Okay, we can go now."

As they passed through the door and out into the cold late November air, Wade caught a glimpse of his rival, Philippe, watching them from the foyer as they departed.

Back at the apartment, Gabriella quickly said goodnight and disappeared abruptly into her room. Wade looked at his watch – it was after four o'clock in the morning. In spite of being extremely tired after the day's exertions he was unable to switch off. The strobe lighting had disturbed him and the noise of the disco had left him with a ringing sound in his ears. When he finally fell asleep, he dreamt that Gabriella had been working in England and he was driving her to the airport to catch her plane back home. He didn't want her to leave.

*

He eventually emerged in the late morning, only to find that Gabriella and Marina had already gone out. The weather had changed. There had been some snow in the night and it was a chilly day. Wade was concerned that he wasn't adequately equipped for cold weather or for heavy rain. He needed a warm winter jacket, good thermal underwear and a poncho.

He enquired at the city information office and they directed him to a specialist store nearby, where the sales clerk advised him and helped him spend quite a lot of money. But the quality was good.

When he tried on a poncho, which had enough room at the back to cover his backpack too, he looked doubtfully at his reflection in the mirror.

"It doesn't look very elegant," he said.

The sales clerk laughed. "My friend, it's not a beauty competition, but this poncho will at least keep you dry."

After a light lunch in a bar near the cathedral square, Wade returned to the apartment and collected his dirty laundry. At the main halls of residence, there were washing machines and also internet facilities and he planned to catch up with his emails while his laundry was being done. When he went online, he found there was an email for him from Danilo, who had met up with Maja again in León, but they had left the day before and were by now well on their way to Astorga.

He had not yet sent an update to Angelina, sweet Angelina, so he wrote an email to her:

Hi Angelina

We got to León at last and are staying at the albergue José de Unamuno, right near the magnificent cathedral here. I've been walking with Gabriella and Marina (from Italy) for a couple of days and we will be here until tomorrow, which gives me time to catch up on my emails.

It's good that you're happy to be with your family and colleagues again. What do you think you got from the Camino?

Our conversation on the last night in Burgos was for me quite mind-blowing. I have never been questioned like that before and I certainly never answered probing questions so frankly to anyone before. You made me realise what I'd been missing all these years and it had a profound emotional effect on me. Then, next day, when I got your message as I walked alone on the empty Meseta, I was kind of happy that you had written to me and not just disappeared without trace, sad because I was too old for you, sorry that I had wasted so many years of potential relationships by refusing to allow my heart to search for a new love. These and the Camino itself combined to overwhelm me for a while.

I think I've come to terms with things now and while you won't be the whole Camino to me, you will remain an important part of it. I hope we will remain friends and that we'll meet again one day. In the meantime, I will continue to let you know how my Camino adventure is going.

With love

Wade x

As he was leaving the hall of residence with his clean laundry, he noticed Carlos and Philippe hanging out in reception. So, they were still in town. Wade wondered if he would see Gabriella again in the evening. He sent her a message:

Are you girls having dinner tonight, or are you otherwise engaged? I don't want to feel like a lemon.

He drank a cup of coffee at the apartment and considered his situation. He was confused. How could he try to get involved with Gabriella when he had already lost his heart to Angelina? He decided there and then to visit the cathedral and seek guidance.

The impressive cathedral in León was very busy with tourists everywhere, some in groups with a guide, others listening to a commentary on their headsets, many taking photos and admiring the famous, stained glass windows – but Wade needed a peaceful place for contemplation and prayer. Finally, in an annexe to the main cathedral, away from the crowds, he found a quiet chapel. He entered a pew towards the front and knelt down, looking at the altar at first, trying to get his mind under control. Then he closed his eyes.

"O God, my God, whoever you are, wherever you are, whatever you are, I need your guidance," he prayed. "But first of all, I must thank you for taking good care of me and getting me safely this far on my amazing journey. My body is standing up to the challenge and I feel like a young man again. For this I am grateful and I will never forget this time till my dying day."

He felt tears trickling down his face and paused for a moment to dry his eyes with a tissue.

"But I think I'm losing track of my goal for this Camino – to seek a direction for the rest of my life in order to find... to find you, my God. Help me, please!"

After some minutes he stood up and made his way from the chapel and departed through the main building into the square in front of the cathedral. He strolled over to the large, bronze León sign, where for once there was nobody having their picture taken, and turned to look back at the imposing cathedral he had just left, with its pale, yellow stone facade framed by two asymmetrical towers. As he stood there, he sensed a familiar presence beside him.

"Hola," said the old Diego. "You've made it as far as León, which is good, but you are troubled. Perhaps your pilgrimage is not turning out as you had expected?"

Wade nodded.

"That's normal," said the old man. "There is a saying, and it's true, that the Camino gives you what you need, not what you want."

"I've heard this already," said Wade. "But aren't they the same thing?"

"Many people think so, but with fortitude, you may understand the difference in the end. In the meantime follow the arrows and experience what you must until you find the truth." Diego paused for a moment before adding: "Your inner self will be examined, there will be temptations and suffering, highs and lows, maybe even revelations. It is how you deal with all these that will determine your ultimate Camino experience."

Even as he was considering what Diego meant by these words, the old man had vanished.

Wade walked slowly back to the apartment, glad of his warm, new winter jacket in the cold, early evening air. Things had to change. He would start in the morning with some serious walking and a new attitude. Enough with pretending to himself that he was young again, chasing after girls, like all those decades ago in Greece. The next day was Sunday. He would leave alone, trying to make a reasonably early start.

He had only been back at the apartment a few minutes when Gabriella arrived.

"I got your message," she said. "But I couldn't reply because my phone needs topping up. Then I called round earlier this afternoon, but you had gone out."

"Yes, I was at the cathedral."

"How was it?"

"Very impressive, but very crowded too. But I managed to find a quiet chapel and I said a few prayers." He paused before adding: "It's only the second time in about fifty years."

Gabriella looked at him quizzically. "Be careful what you pray for. You could get hurt."

Wade wondered what she meant by that. Did she think he had been praying for her love?

"We're all meeting up at the León sign in front of the cathedral at eight o'clock and then going on to a restaurant," Gabriella continued.

"Okay, I'll be there."

"By the way, what do you mean by 'being a lemon'?"

"Well, I was uncomfortable when we met up in the bar last night. You were with Philippe, Marina was with Carlos and I was the odd one out – the lemon."

"Hmmm… Did you feel like that all night?"

"No, I didn't. Later on, at the disco, it was better," said Wade. But to be honest about it, he hadn't really enjoyed that very much either.

Gabriella soon left again and Wade rested on the sofa in the lounge area. Marina was now staying at the main hall of residence where she could be with Carlos and before long Wade met a new resident at the apartment, a middle-aged Spaniard who had taken over Marina's old room. Then shortly afterwards he had something of a shock when Philippe arrived, complete with backpack, to occupy the fourth room in the apartment at the far end of the corridor – a room that had not been available the day before. This was beginning to feel like being part of a French bedroom farce.

Shortly before eight o'clock, Wade got ready to leave the apartment again. The short walk through the dark, narrow streets to the cathedral square took no more than five minutes and he arrived at the León sign before any of the others. The evening air was chilly and he was glad of his new jacket. Richard and Julie were the next to arrive together with a young Swedish couple that he remembered from the group in Sahagún, then Philippe, Carlos and Marina, and finally Gabriella.

"Wow! Tonight is where our first family comes to an end and a second one forms," she said. "It's very interesting to see how it just happens."

Wade didn't tell her for the moment about his plans to leave alone the next day. He didn't want to be part of this new pilgrim family. There was nothing that could replace his first family, the one he had walked with till Burgos.

After some discussion, they went to an Italian restaurant near the store where Wade had bought his new winter clothing. As on the previous evening, he found himself at the opposite end of the table to Gabriella, having once again been outmanoeuvred by Philippe. It was a good meal, but Wade didn't really enjoy it. Somehow he didn't feel part of this scene. There were private conversations in Italian or Spanish, almost everyone had a smartphone on the table, which they were constantly tapping on and sending one another secret messages (or so it seemed to him) and in between times they were all taking pictures of each other, pictures of the group, pictures of the food. He found it irritating. What was he doing with these people? He was more determined than ever to get away the following morning.

Late in the evening, they all walked back to the main square together. The young Swedish couple were flying back home the following day, so there were big hugs all round and a blitz of photographs. Wade set his features in a kind of grimace and waited impatiently for the evening to end.

He eventually managed to get Gabriella's attention as they finally made their way back to the main hall of residence. They walked side by side.

"There's something I have to tell you tonight," he said. "I've decided to go on by myself early tomorrow morning and maybe try to catch Danilo up or some of the others from my first family."

"Why?"

"I don't feel that I belong with your group, with this constant picture taking and phone messages all the time. It really gets me down."

"Hmmm… I think I understand why you want to catch Danilo up," Gabriella said eventually.

Wade wondered to himself what she meant by that. "I've enjoyed meeting you, Gabriella. I hope you'll keep in contact and that we'll meet again along the way."

"We'll meet again. That's for sure," she said.

"Yes, in the meantime I'll leave you to your guys."

"What do you mean – my guys?" She sounded angry.

"You know, Carlos and Philippe, that's who I mean." He paused for a moment, before adding: "Actually, Carlos is okay, but I don't much like Philippe."

He looked down at her face, and she had one of those enigmatic smiles that had first attracted his interest. "Philippe can be fun," she said. "He knows how to make me laugh."

At the entrance to the main building, Richard and Julie said goodnight, as did Marina, and the three of them went inside.

"Wait for me here please, I won't be long," said

Gabriella to Wade, before she too disappeared into the building.

Wade was left standing in the street outside, where Philippe spoke secretively to Carlos in French, saying something about going to the disco again instead of sleeping with Gabriella, mistakenly thinking Wade would not understand. Then, Carlos said goodnight and went inside the building while Philippe headed off alone.

Wade smiled to himself. Obviously, Gabriella had rejected the Swiss guy's advances.

He waited patiently for about ten minutes before Gabriella reappeared.

"You've been waiting for me all this time?" she said.

"Of course. You asked me to wait, so I waited."

"Sorry I was so long. I was talking to Richard and Julie."

They walked together in silence through the darkened streets back to their apartment. When they got there, Gabriella went straight to her room. Philippe was preparing to go out again.

"Have a nice time!" he said to Wade, somewhat sarcastically, as he swept out of the apartment.

Alone at last with Gabriella, Wade thought this must be the opportune moment he had been waiting for. If so, how would he manage without Viagra? It could be embarrassing. The door of Gabriella's room opened and she came towards him.

"I will say goodnight now," she said. "I'm very tired. You will probably be gone before I get up tomorrow."

When she kissed him lightly on both cheeks, he tried gently to draw her towards him, but she resisted with her hands firmly on his shoulders, keeping him at a distance. With a final, "Goodnight!" she turned and went back into her room.

Wade retired to his own room. His mind was racing and he couldn't sleep. Had he messed up his chances when he told her he was leaving and that he was irritated by her *peregrino* family? Or was he just a silly old man, whose wishful thinking was reading too much into every situation?

He put the light on and wrote a short note to Gabriella, which he pushed under her door.

Dear Gabriella

I enjoyed our time together on the way to León, but these last two evenings with your reformed, enlarged 'family' have not been much fun for me and I've hardly had a chance to speak to you. Perhaps it's because, not being a member of the smartphone secret society, I'm usually the last person to know what's going on.

I think one or two days by myself may be a good thing, but I really do hope we'll meet up again on the way and I can get to know you better.

Today I'm planning to reach Villadangos del Paramo and then go on to Astorga tomorrow, but plans can change and I'll text you my progress.

Take care.

Wade x

Then he went back to bed but slept only fitfully. At about four o'clock he heard the entrance door to the apartment open and close, then the sound of footsteps along the corridor as Philippe returned from the disco and went to his room.

6. SPIRIT

The guidebook's recommended route, via Villar de Mazarife, would have been a more interesting way, but Wade didn't care about the scenery after he left León. Instead, he followed the rather monotonous, unattractive main road route towards Villadangos del Paramo, anxious just to move on and leave the big city well behind him. He walked by himself the whole day, alone with his thoughts, alone with his feelings.

Why had he got so uptight in León? Why had he felt pangs of jealousy when he saw Gabriella and Philippe together? How could he, a pensioner, possibly compete with a randy, forty-year-old Swiss anyway? He hardly knew Gabriella, they had no obligations to each other, it really didn't matter – so why all the sweat? Of course, he was interested, but not in the same way as with Angelina. Pursuing Gabriella was more like a game really, just like all those decades ago when he was in Greece...

He had been miserable for a long time after Tamsin's departure for America, working hard but not enjoying it, drinking too much, sleeping badly. Eventually, throwing caution to the winds, he had put his career on hold and taken a sabbatical. At least, that was the official version of life after Tasmin, the story that he had propagated, but was it true? Now, nearly forty years later, he almost believed it himself; but in reality, it was losing his job, after the affair with Amy, that had led to his dropping out.

He had spent the summer in Greece, living out of a rucksack and staying at youth hostels. Then one day he had stumbled across this hostel in the pine woods, near a village by the sea, just up the coast from Athens, where he had become friendly with some young Greek guys who had been hanging out there and chasing after the girls who came to the hostel. After some initial reticence, he had pushed his recent experiences deep into the back of his mind and joined them. But he was shy and reserved – not a natural playboy like the others.

"Don't give up too easy, Wade," his friend Stelios told him. "These girls are here for a good time too. You've got to keep trying."

And it had worked.

Then one day Sabina, a sun-tanned German girl with blue eyes and long blonde hair, had arrived. She was on her way back to Frankfurt after spending six months at a Kibbutz in Israel, and he had fallen for her, and she for him.

He plodded on, passing through Villadangos del Paramo until he reached San Martin del Camino, an undistinguished village stretching out along the main road. He finally stopped at a private albergue that advertised internet on the billboard outside.

There were very few people staying at the albergue, which was cold and depressing. Perhaps in the season it would be okay, but now at the start of winter the facilities had been reduced to a minimum – the internet wasn't working, the shower was barely lukewarm and there was no heating in the dormitory.

"It's like a cemetery with lights," Wade muttered to himself.

Maybe he should have checked out again, but having paid in advance for dinner and breakfast, as well as his bunk for the night, he didn't want to lose his money. He went out to look for a bar in the village and found one about ten minutes further along the main road. From outside it didn't appear very inviting, but it was warm, busy and cheerful when he went upstairs into the bar and he wished he could stay there the whole night. He drank a little red wine followed by several schnapps and sent a couple of texts. The first was to Gabriella:

In san martin del camino. Very quiet. A bit lonely. Tomorrow astorga. Wade x

The other one was to Angelina:

Left leon today. Walked 27km to san martin del camino. Cold and lonely. Miss you.

Love Wade x

He returned to the chilly albergue for dinner and

went to bed soon afterwards. With thick socks, two layers of thermal underwear and a blanket, he was just about able to cope with the icy cold air in the dormitory. Outside it was freezing hard and inside it wasn't much warmer.

He lay there in his bunk, unable to sleep. *What have I done?* he thought.

He had cut the bonds to his new pilgrim family and was now quite alone on the Camino, and he didn't like it. He would be glad to get it over with and go home, but he wouldn't give in. He tried to be optimistic, just hoping, like Mr Micauber, that something would turn up. Could he mend bridges? He didn't know any more.

In any case, should he not be looking inward at the Self, rather than seeking the company of others for support? It was an emotional time. Could he handle it alone? He needed help.

His mobile phone was under his pillow and he heard it buzzing in his ear. It was a message from Angelina:

Cheer up! You're doing fine. Tomorrow will be better. Big hug. Angelina x

"Thank you," he whispered.

*

Morning came at last. Wade's neighbour in the albergue, a middle-aged Spaniard in the next bunk, spoke to him as they packed their bags ready to leave.

"This is very, very bad albergue," he said with feeling. Wade could only agree.

Unexpectedly, breakfast was quite good and there

was even some semblance of heating in the dining room, so Wade was in a cheerier frame of mind when he left the albergue and began his day's walk to Astorga. Though the sun was shining brightly, the air was cold and the clock-thermometer outside the local pharmacy was registering minus two degrees Celsius as he walked past. Then, clearing the village, he noticed that the fields were all white with frost.

After about an hour's walk, Wade reached the lovely medieval bridge, with its many arches, that crosses the river into Hospital de Órbigo. He stopped at a bar near the bridge and sent a text message to Angelina as he ate his second breakfast of the day:

Last night was a crisis. Very cold in albergue. Depressing, but your text cheered me up. Thank you. Love. Wade x

He also sent a message to Gabriella.

Hi Gabriella, i fear i may have offended you in leon, which was not my intention. I would like to be friends, so i hope you will contact me. Wade x

As he was finishing his coffee, another pilgrim entered the bar and joined him at his table. He was a man in his forties from Portugal and was rather more smartly dressed than the average pilgrim.

"I walk mainly alone," he told Wade, "so I can enjoy the landscape, the architecture and the history along the way, but I don't meet so many people."

"With me, it's the opposite," said Wade. "I miss many of the fine views because I am talking, listening or thinking about relationships. It's not what I'd planned, but it's how it's worked out so far."

"Do you stay at the albergues?"

"Yes usually, because it's there that I meet up with people I already know, or make new friends."

"I tried it," said the pilgrim from Portugal, "but it was impossible to sleep in the crowded albergues, with all that snoring, and they can be a bit primitive. So now I stay mainly at private hostels where I can get a room for myself, or share with only one or two others."

Wade considered this for a moment before he spoke. "Although we're walking the same route, our Caminos are really quite different."

From Órbigo to Astorga Wade took the scenic route, a distance of about sixteen kilometres, rather than following the main road as he had done the previous day. He was rewarded by a lovely rolling landscape, with pleasant woodlands, all bathed in the late autumn sunshine. He took his time. It was early in the day and he only had a short stretch ahead of him. After a gentle climb, he stopped to rest in the shade of a tree adjacent to the path and admired the view below, listening to the soft sounds of nature. Abruptly, the buzz of his mobile phone broke the silence. It was a very brief text from Gabriella:

There! Phone topped up and working again :)

So that was why he hadn't heard from her since León – maybe she cared a little bit after all. He walked on until, near the top of the hill a few kilometres short of Astorga, he saw a dilapidated stone barn with what looked like a kiosk standing in front of it, next to the way. He noticed a few items of fruit and some drinks on display. Nearby, sitting cross-legged on a bench under a canopy giving some shelter from the elements, were two young men dressed in loose-fitting garments reminiscent of Asia. They looked up from the books they were reading as he approached.

"An oasis!" Wade called out as he drew near.

"Welcome! Come and rest for a while," they replied.

There was room on the bench for a third person, so he took off his backpack and joined them. The beam supporting the front of the canopy was quite low. "Mind your head!" said the younger of the two men as Wade sat down.

Wade stayed there, talking with them for about an hour. He also drank some tea, which they provided at their kiosk. "There is no charge," said the younger man, "but if you want to leave a donation you can."

They talked about meditation. "I went on a meditation retreat for a week last year," said Wade. "It was interesting, but I felt that for me it was like trying to meditate, but not quite succeeding."

"How much did you pay for this course?"

"Oh, I don't remember exactly, but including accommodation and meals it was well over £200."

"That's a lot of money. You can stay here with us, and we will teach you for nothing."

For a moment Wade was almost tempted, but he had his own path to follow. "Thank you, but I must continue my Camino to the end."

Just before he left, Wade asked the two men if they had seen Danilo. He began to describe Danilo's appearance, but it wasn't necessary.

"Your friend stopped and talked with us two days ago. He was with a young woman. She was beautiful."

"That would be Maja."

"Yes, that was her name."

Wade said goodbye and continued on his way, after first putting a few coins into the donation box at the kiosk.

It wasn't long before he reached the Cruceiro de Santo Toribio – a stone cross standing on an open plateau, looking down on the town of Astorga below, and beyond it to the mysterious heights of the Montes de León on the horizon. The magnificent view, enhanced by the sunshine, lifted his heart as he made his way down the hill and towards the town.

The municipal albergue was on one side of a pleasant square near the entrance to the town. There was a statue of a pilgrim in the centre of the square and nearby, in the sunshine, stood a bench. Wade sat down to rest for a few minutes before checking in. He had found from experience that he often felt quite groggy and a little vague at the end of the day's walk, so it was generally better to gather his wits about him before conducting any negotiations with the hospitalero.

The albergue had all the basic facilities, including a kitchen for the pilgrims' use and internet computers. Wade was allocated a top bunk in a small dormitory on the ground floor. The other pilgrims who had suffered at the bad albergue the night before were there too, and he saw some of the León crowd in the corridor, but Gabriella's pilgrim family was not there – at least not yet.

A fair-haired woman in his room caught his eye and he thought she was English at first, her accent was so authentic, but she turned out to be Danish and her name was Katrine. She was not very tall, but quite sporty-looking and Wade guessed she was in her late thirties.

"Are you walking alone?" he asked her.

"I was alone at the beginning, but now I'm with those French guys." She indicated three young men in the opposite corner of the room.

After Wade had showered and changed his clothes he went to the computers in the lobby to check his emails. There was one from Danilo:

Hola Wade!

How are you now? In Astorga, is very nice hotel called Via de la Plata! Was there with Maja. Double room is 70 euro with breakfast! Otherwise the albergue municipal is 5 euro.

Bye

Danilo

Wade replied right away:

Hi Danilo

I arrived in Astorga today. I'm sure you and Maja enjoyed your stay in style at the hotel.

I'm at the municipal albergue. The two guys with a kind of kiosk, meditating on the mountain, told me they saw you a couple of days ago. They asked me if I wanted to stay and join them, but I'm not ready for that lifestyle just yet.

I'm in contact with Gabriella, though I'm not sure if I offended her when I decided to go on alone for a while. Hope to see her later. She's a nice young lady, but maybe a bit devious.

I've been getting regular messages from Angelina, which I am very happy to receive. She really is a special person and I hope we will remain friends.

I don't think I'm likely to catch up before Santiago, but with luck, I will see you both there.

Keep in touch.

Wade

There was nothing new from Angelina, but her text message the night before was fresh in his mind. He wrote to her:

Hi Angelina

I arrived in Astorga today, travelling alone for the moment. It's a new experience. Last night was very cold and I nearly froze to death. Your text message kept me alive I think :) Fortunately, the municipal albergue here in Astorga seems OK and I should at least be warm enough.

Gradually getting a few Facebook friends. Particularly glad to have you as one of them. Of course, Facebook is still something of a mystery to me and I won't get much chance to use it while I'm on the Camino, but it will give me the chance of keeping in touch with peregrino friends when I get back home.

I'm tempted to have an extra day's 'holiday' here in Astorga. I'll see how I feel in the morning.

Keep in touch. Let me know how you are getting on.

With love

Wade x

He had decided to take advantage of the kitchen facilities at the albergue and cook for himself that evening, so when he had finished his emails he went into Astorga to look at the town and buy food. There was a well-stocked supermarket not far away and he was tempted to buy a lot of good things, but on reflection, he bought only essentials for a simple evening meal, including of course a bottle of red wine. There was no sense in buying more because he had no way of carrying it. His backpack was already full to bursting point.

Wade wondered what had happened to Gabriella. It was getting late and there was no sign of her or her family when he got back to the albergue. He sent her a text:

Gabriella, i am in municipal albergue in astorga. Where are you?

The kitchen at the albergue was busy, but he managed to get his meal ready fairly quickly. It was basically a matter of opening cans of food and heating the contents. He sat at the large table in the adjacent dining area, where a clean-cut, Australian couple and a red-bearded, wild-looking young man were already sitting. As they talked together, it soon became clear to Wade that the young man with the red beard could only be from Texas. His name was Luke and he had served as a paramedic in the US army in Afghanistan, but he was now a civilian once more and celebrating his newfound freedom.

As Wade was returning to his dormitory, he met Gabriella and her family in the corridor. It was almost ten o'clock, but they had only just arrived and were about to go down to the kitchen to cook and eat their evening meal. Gabriella's greeting was friendly enough.

"Hola Wade. Would you like to eat with us?"

"Thanks, Gabriella, it's kind of you, but I've eaten already. How come you're so late?"

"We didn't start very early and it's been slow going today because of my blisters. I can hardly walk at the moment."

Wade exchanged a few words of greeting with the others, though Philippe didn't look particularly pleased to see him again, and then he went to bed. He wanted to make an early start in the morning and also visit the cathedral in Astorga before moving on.

*

After a decent night's sleep, he should have felt good to be alive when he woke the next morning, but he didn't. There were few people around as he strolled up through the town to the cathedral. The reddish hue of its sandstone facade contrasted nicely with the surrounding paved areas, white with frost, and he would normally have viewed this as an attractive setting. But the cathedral was locked shut and he had to wait for quite some time until the doors were opened to visitors. So much for his early start, he reflected moodily.

He went to a pew facing the altar and knelt down to pray. There was his usual difficulty of not knowing who he was praying to, and though he wanted to believe, as he had once believed as a child, this simple faith was missing.

"Oh God, whoever you are, whatever you are, I thank you for bringing me this far on my pilgrimage. It is a physical challenge for me but that's not a huge problem, at least not yet. The real problems are in my mind and in my heart. I came to find my faith and a new direction for the rest of my life, but I seem to have… to have fallen by the wayside, as the bible would say. Instead of seeking my God, I've been tempted to chase after women, young women, because Angelina made me realise what I have missed all these years. Now here I am, getting old but imagining that I am young again. It will surely end badly, I know, but I can't help it somehow. It can only bring me suffering and heartache. There's no fool like an old fool and that's a fact. Help me to keep going at all costs, however stupid I am, so that in the end I may find the truth."

Filled with emotion, as he so often was along the way, he left the cathedral in tears and pressed on, looking only for signs of shells and yellow arrows to guide him and oblivious to the sights and sounds of nature. As the graffiti on walls and waymarks often reminded him, the Camino was a rollercoaster with its ups and downs, and at the moment he was at a low point.

In contemplative mood, Wade walked steadily on along a rutted track that curved to the right to go past an isolated farmhouse and barn, which were the only buildings in sight in an otherwise empty landscape. All was quiet with not a soul to be seen, until suddenly, as he neared the entrance to the open barn, he was startled by the sight and sound of two large, angry dogs. He had come across many barking dogs along the way, either tethered to a stake in the ground or enclosed behind a sturdy fence. Who wouldn't be angry in such a situation? He felt sorry for the imprisoned animals. But these two were different – they were running free.

They came charging out of the barn and faced him on the track, just a few metres ahead, barring his way. Wade sensed that these two black beasts, with their glaring eyes and menacing snarls, posed a real threat and he wished he had walking poles or at least a stick to fend them off with.

Not for the first time was Wade reminded of the devil dog in Paulo Coelho's book. It was important to show no fear. If he tried to run for it or turned his back to the dogs they would surely attack him. He stopped where he was, motionless, facing them down, his heart beating wildly. It seemed an age that they stood like this before the farmer eventually came out of the house to see what all the noise was about and called the dogs off. Only then did Wade feel safe enough to turn his back on the scene and walk briskly on, but it was some time before his heartbeat returned to normal.

He walked quickly now, wrapped in his own gloomy thoughts, only occasionally slowing or stopping to have a few words with the other pilgrims that he encountered along the way. He got the impression that most of them would continue as far as Foncebadón. He decided to send a text to Gabriella, for although he had Angelina in his heart he also felt physically attracted to Gabriella, as a mouse with whiskers twitching is attracted to a piece of cheese that is just out of reach. He didn't want to lose touch with her.

Going on to rabanal del camino or maybe further today, and you? Wade x

The reply came just a few minutes later.

Taking care of blisters. You'll find the others at your destination. Buen camino

Wade walked on for a while, thinking about what he should do next. When Gabriella talked about 'the others', did this mean Philippe too? If so, she was probably alone in Astorga. Maybe this was another opportune moment and he didn't want to risk missing it. He was just approaching Rabanal del Camino and though it was only early in the afternoon he gave up any idea of continuing to Foncebadón and made up his mind to stop here.

The albergue in Rabanal, which was run by the Confraternity of Saint James, was situated opposite a small church in the centre of the village. He was welcomed by Dave, one of the volunteer hospitaleros.

"You're the first of the day," said Dave, "and you may be the only pilgrim we have tonight."

"There are quite a lot of pilgrims behind me. I don't think they'll all go on to Foncebadón."

"Well, in any case, you have the choice of bunks. I can recommend the one nearest to the chimney stack because you get some of the heat from the fire downstairs transferred through the bricks. It's going to be a cold night."

"Thanks for the tip. By the way, is there any chance of an extra blanket? My sleeping bag isn't very thick."

"No problem. My colleague, Alison, is upstairs now and I'm sure she'll fix you up with a couple of blankets."

"Have you got a washing machine? I really need to wash some things."

"No, but you can wash clothes in the basins in the yard outside. We have a really good spin dryer, plus there's a washing line in the garden and the sun shines there till quite late."

Wade was doubtful if they would dry in the late November sunshine, but one of the problems with travelling light was the need to be constantly washing clothes. He decided to take a chance.

A while later, just as he returned from hanging out his clothes on the line in the sunny garden, two more pilgrims came up to the albergue, and he recognised the familiar faces of Carlos and Marina.

There was no sign of Philippe, so Wade assumed he had stayed behind in Astorga with Gabriella. This was disappointing, of course, but he realised that he had been too much alone recently and greeted Carlos and Marina as old friends. The three of them went to the village store and bought some food for the evening because the albergue had a well-equipped kitchen and Carlos enjoyed cooking. But first, there was an opportunity to take part in a service at the tiny Romanesque church opposite the albergue.

"If there are two priests it will be sung vespers at seven o'clock," Alison told them. "I can recommend it. It's very beautiful. If there is only one priest, there will just be a spoken mass. But the tiny church is lovely, and in any case, it is a moving experience."

They decided to go to the church and cook afterwards.

The building was furnished simply, with little of the ornate decoration that Wade had seen in churches or cathedrals along the way. There were only a few rows of pews, all facing the altar, and he entered a pew on the opposite side of the nave to Carlos and Marina who were sitting together. He looked around and saw just a handful of local people in the congregation, including Alison from the albergue who was sitting in the back row.

At seven o'clock a solitary priest entered through the vestry door and the mass began. It occurred to Wade that he had not taken communion for very many years – not since his youth in fact. He was unsure if the mass was spoken in Spanish or Latin – he knew little or nothing of either language. He kept an eye open to see when the person in the pew in front of him stood up, or sat down, or kneeled, and he did likewise. Then, when it came to the sacrament and the priest gave him the token bread, he was astonished to hear the words being spoken to him in English – "The body of our Lord Jesus Christ." It was another emotional moment for Wade.

After the mass, Wade and his friends returned to the albergue, where there had been a number of new arrivals. A group of young Spaniards had arrived, some of them on bikes, and the party also included a couple of punkish looking girls, with nose rings and heavily tattooed. They had wine and they were noisy but friendly enough. Wade wondered if they would all be in for a sleepless night.

Late in the evening, who should arrive but Philippe – alone. So he hadn't stayed with Gabriella in Astorga after all. Wade went into the garden in the darkness and sent Gabriella a text.

Really sorry about the blisters. I'm in rabanal. Are you ok? Can wait for you if you want. Wade x

Why was he doing this, he wondered? One moment he was trying to find his God and the next attempting, once again, to compete with Philippe for the favours of a woman young enough to be his daughter. It was perverse, but he couldn't help himself.

After a noisy evening drinking wine with the punks, they all retired upstairs to the dormitory. It was a cold night, but Wade, whose bunk was next to the warm chimney breast and with the extra blankets that Alison had given him, was plenty warm enough. To his surprise, everyone was quiet, even the punks, and he slept well till the morning.

*

They had breakfast in the kitchen at the albergue before setting off up the hill towards the ruins of Foncebadón. It was bitter cold, with a thick layer of ice on every patch of water. Philippe was present in body but not in spirit, as he kept trying to get in touch with Gabriella.

"I expect she's with those Canadians," said Philippe somewhat bitterly. He was speaking more to Carlos than to Wade. "I saw the way that Richard looked at her in Astorga."

"Well, she's an attractive woman," said Wade. "I like her too, but she's very elusive."

"Ah, another one for the Gabriella fan club," said Philippe, and they all laughed. "Yes, she is very attractive. I was with her in Burgos and it was fantastic."

They stopped for a rest and a second breakfast when they reached the albergue in Foncebadón. There was a welcoming fire burning in the hearth and the atmosphere was cosy and friendly. Wade recognised two young Germans he had met at the albergue in Astorga. Both of them were called Sebastian and both carried guitars.

"This is a great place to stay," said the slighter of the two Sebastians, a fair-haired youth in his late teens. "We were up till late, a whole group of us, singing together and playing guitar."

They were reluctant to leave the blazing fire and go out again onto the wintry hillside; but when they set off once more, Wade noticed that among the ruins of Foncebadón some of the derelict houses were being rebuilt. He was reminded of something he had read in Paulo Coelho's book, but he couldn't for the moment remember what it was. While his companions plodded on up the hill, he paused to think and became aware of a familiar figure at his shoulder. It was Diego.

"I wondered when you would appear again," said Wade.

"I'm never far away," replied the old man mysteriously. "It was here in the ruins of Foncebadón that Paulo Coelho overcame the demon of the road."

"Ah yes, I remember now," said Wade. "The ferocious devil dog. His name was Legion and when he was defeated, the power left here would enable Foncebadón to rise again from the ruins one day. And look! It's happening now."

"Indeed!" said Diego. "But you have some way to go before you overcome your demon of the road."

"My demon?"

"Yes, the demon that is interfering with your spiritual search."

"Are you suggesting that Angelina is my demon, or even Gabriella?"

"Of course not. Your demon is within you, but you have some more lessons to learn before you realise this. Each step along the way and each experience brings you nearer to the truth."

They had reached the top of the ruined village by this time. "We'll meet again soon," said Diego, indicating to Wade that he should continue without him. Wade turned to face the uphill climb again and without looking back he walked on towards the next target – the famous Cruz de Ferro.

He caught the others up and they walked steadily on until the Cruz de Ferro came into sight. Wade had imagined it to be positioned in isolated magnificence at the top of a lonely, windswept mountain, so the reality, with its car park and picnic area came as something of an anticlimax. He was glad to be walking in late November because at least they had the place to themselves and it was impressive enough for everyone to take too many photos. Wade noticed that Philippe had brought a stone with him to add to the pile surrounding the monument. A wish or a prayer for Gabriella maybe?

The pilgrims were blessed by the sun, as usual, but at nearly 1,500 metres above sea level, the air was cold. Wade was very glad he had bought new thermal underwear and a padded jacket in León. They were really necessary now.

The four of them were there for some time, taking more and more pictures of the Cruz de Ferro when suddenly they heard a cheery, "Hola!" and Richard and Julie came marching by. They were greeted a little coolly by the others, but Wade quite liked the Canadian couple and decided to walk on with them for the moment.

"Where did you spend last night?" said Wade. He was really fishing for any information about Gabriella's whereabouts.

"We slept at a pension in Rabanal," said Richard. "Julie wanted a bit of comfort after all those albergues. She's finding it hard going at present."

They looked around and saw that Julie had already dropped some way behind.

"I'd better wait for her here," Richard continued. "We'll probably stop for the day if we can find a pension in one of the next villages."

"Okay!" said Wade. "Then I'll see you later. I want to reach the municipal albergue in Molinaseca today, so I'll press on now. Buen Camino!"

He continued on his way, making a slight detour from the marked track to climb up to the highest point on the Camino, near the Cruce Militar, where a stone cairn marked the spot at more than 1,500 metres above sea level. Wade made a quick mental calculation. That must be quite a bit higher than Ben Nevis, which surprised him. Wow! He had this summit to himself and he rested there for a while in the sunshine, enjoying the spectacular views stretching across the heather-strewn hills and valleys to the mysterious grey peaks on the distant horizon. Then, feeling refreshed, he descended the rocky path to rejoin the waymarked route, eventually arriving in the village of Molinaseca.

He sat on a bench facing the river and checked his guidebook to see where the albergue was situated. Below him, near the riverbank, were two other pilgrims. They were the first he had seen since leaving Richard and Julie on the mountainside. One of the pilgrims he recognised as Enrique, a tall, good-looking, young Argentinian in his early twenties he had seen at the disco in León, and the other was a pretty girl he was trying to impress. Wade smiled to himself a little ruefully, wishing for the moment that he was young again. He hadn't checked for messages since leaving the Cruz de Ferro, so now he looked and saw that he had received a text from Gabriella. His heart nearly missed a beat.

Hi, thx for yr notes. All good w me, taking time for myself. Will continue at my pace. Wish you well and great camino.

Well, at least she had written to him. He sent a reply.

Good to hear you are well. I'm in molinaseca tonight. Where are you? See you in santiago? Take care. Wade x

He had rested enough. It was time to move on and find the albergue. He crossed the ancient Roman bridge, with its many arches, over the Meruelo River and into the village. Then he had to walk right through the quiet village before eventually reaching the municipal albergue. Even though the door was open there was nobody about, but he went inside anyway and found a large room with steps down to the main communal area in the centre. It reminded him of pictures he had seen of the old Roman baths. There was also a gas fireplace in the central area, but the room was very cold as the fire was not lit. A table, chairs and simple cooking facilities completed the scene. But where was the sleeping accommodation? Two flights of steps led to the first floor and there he found a lot of bunks and blankets, but it looked as though he was the first pilgrim of the day. He left his backpack upstairs and went down to the ground floor again. Here he saw a door leading off to the toilets and showers. It was all fairly basic, but it would be okay if only the place was warm.

After a few more minutes the main door opened and the hospitalero entered. As Wade was checking in, he noticed that the register showed eleven pilgrims the night before, but at the moment it looked as if he might be the only one that night. The hospitalero lit the fire, said he would be back later and disappeared again. Slowly, slowly, the place began to warm up.

After he had showered, changed and sorted out his bedding, Wade sent Angelina a message:

Made it to molinaseca today. Albergue ok but no internet. About 8 days to santiago now. How about a short holiday there with opa :-). Wade x

He had just sent the message when he heard the sound of the albergue door being opened below and then footsteps coming up the stairs. It was Philippe.

"Is there nobody else here?" he asked.

"No, just me. The hospitalero was here earlier, but he went again and said he would come back later."

Philippe looked around him doubtfully, clearly considering whether to stay or not, but after a few minutes of contemplation he chose a bunk and unpacked his things. Not long afterwards Marina and Carlos arrived, but with no sign yet of the missing hospitalero. Philippe was growing restless.

"I don't want to wait for this man forever," he said. "I'm going back into the town to find a bar with Wi-Fi, so I can try to contact Gabriella. I will check in here when I return."

After he left, the other three decided to make use of the cooking facilities and prepare their evening meal themselves. Wade and Carlos walked back into the town to find a supermarket, returning to the albergue some time later with food and wine for the evening meal. Philippe was back already, looking a little despondent at not having been able to contact Gabriella, and in the meantime, another pilgrim had arrived – it was Luke from Texas, with the red beard, last seen in Astorga. But there was no sign of the missing hospitalero.

Carlos and Marina set about preparing the meal, with just a little help from the others. The food was almost ready when the hospitalero turned up at last, signed everybody in, stamped their pilgrim passports with the official stamp, said, "Buenas noches!" and disappeared again. The five pilgrims had the whole albergue to themselves for the night.

Carlos and Marina had prepared a feast and there was plenty of wine too, especially as Philippe had also brought a couple of bottles back from the village. They sat around the table enjoying the food, the wine, the warmth of the gas fire, and the convivial company. The Camino itself was, as always, the main topic of conversation.

"When I get back to Italy, I will frame my Compostela and hang it on the wall," said Marina.

"Some guy told me there are two grades of Compostela certificate," said Texas Luke.

"That's right. If you walk the Camino for spiritual reasons you get a beautiful Compostela in Latin, but if you do it just for fun your Compostela will be in Spanish and maybe not quite so beautiful."

"What!" said Philippe indignantly. "I'm not walking two thousand kilometres for a second-class Compostela. If necessary I will go into the Camino office on my knees, like this."

They laughed as he got down on the ground and shuffled along on his knees.

"I think it's not really a problem," said Carlos. "You just have to tell them it's for spiritual reasons and they'll give you the Latin Compostela without any testing."

"You walked two thousand kilometres?" said Texas Luke. "Wow! Where did you start your Camino?"

"In Geneva, nearly three months ago now."

"That's pretty impressive. You must be very religious."

Marina laughed. "But not since Burgos. Since then

133

Philippe has other matters in his head."

Philippe didn't look amused.

"Yes, Gabriella has become my Camino, I admit it. I don't know where she is now, but I will wait for her in Ponferrada. I think she may be one or two days behind us."

Carlos and Marina planned to spend a night in Ponferrada too, but Wade and Luke wanted to press on. They agreed to leave together early in the morning, while the other three would walk back into Molanaseca for a leisurely breakfast.

That night, as he lay in his bunk in the darkened albergue, Wade thought about Philippe's confession – that the pursuit of Gabriella had become an obsession with him. Did he, Wade, feel the same way about her? No, not really, though he was interested certainly. Besides, in his heart, he knew that Angelina was the one he wanted. Was there a danger that she would be his Camino? He remembered she had warned him against it.

He heard a faint buzzing noise from under his pillow. A message had come through on his mobile phone, and it was from Angelina:

:) Thanks for the idea and invitation, but I'm afraid it won't be the same because I didn't walk it all. Anyway, I'll be in mallorca then with two girlfriends. Hopefully more sun than here. It's raining hard now and getting cold. Missing the spanish sun on my face. Hope you enjoy the snow there, must look beautiful. Take an extra blanket to keep warm at night, take care. x

Snow? They had seen little snow so far – just a sprinkling in León. Had they just missed it at Cruz de

Ferro, or was it still to come? But it was unimportant. He had heard from Angelina, sweet Angelina, and that was all that mattered.

*

Wade and Texas Luke set off after breakfast, walking at a brisk pace to keep warm on a cold day and taking the main road route all the way into the city of Ponferrada. For the moment Wade had lost all interest in his surroundings and just wanted to press on and reach Santiago without undue delay. That was the physical challenge, but he was fit now and short of an unexpected injury it should not be too demanding. The real problems were inside his head. He had a feeling this could be a real rollercoaster day, mentally, and he wanted to be alone so that he could be free to follow his emotions without any inhibitions.

They stopped at a coffee shop in Ponferrada for a second breakfast and afterwards Wade walked on, while his companion stayed for a while to look at the old medieval city around the castle. The weather was not quite so cold as it had been, but rain was threatening all day. Wade trudged on, wrapped in his thoughts, oblivious to his surroundings except for the yellow arrows and waymarks which he registered almost automatically. Many of the waymarks had been adorned with graffiti, some of which echoed his own feelings and reflections.

"What are you searching for?" he read on one waymark.

Good question, he thought. *I wish I knew. Is it sex or salvation?*

Now and then he would burst into tears without any apparent reason. He could not remember a time in his life when he had felt such abrupt emotional ups and downs, but he had heard from other pilgrims, that this feeling was experienced by many on the Camino.

"Roll on, rollercoaster," he read on another waymark.

Eventually, he stopped for a beer at the bar El Molino in the small town of Cacabelos and enquired about accommodation. He didn't feel like walking any further, nor did he want to spend a chilly night in an albergue.

"We've got a room," said the barman, who spoke fluent English, "but I must warn you that there's no heating and it will be cold tonight. Why don't you try the Hostal Santa Maria just down the road? I know they have heated rooms and you will like it there."

Wade finished his beer and went round to the Hostal Santa Maria where he booked a room. After the spartan accommodation of the albergues, it felt like the ultimate in luxury to have a comfortable room of his own, with central heating and bathroom too.

Later on, he returned to El Molino for his evening meal. While he was there he noticed that the bar had internet facilities and he checked his emails to see if there was anything from Angelina. There was. It was in response to the message he had sent her in León just three days before:

Hi Wade

Thanks for writing such an open and honest mail. You know, I didn't mean to pry, but I'm a person with a lot of curiosity. Whenever I meet someone interesting and nice, like you, I like to find out how they think, and how they feel in their heart, so that's why I keep asking questions. I'm very direct, as I told you that last night in Burgos, and I gave you my frank opinion. I'm glad it was of some help.

I was genuinely surprised at what you told me, because you're such a lovely and good looking man. It's difficult to imagine you have been so long without a woman. I'm glad that you were crying after Burgos and didn't try to suppress your emotions. It must have been a relief to allow your feelings to take over.

You asked me what I got from the Camino... Fact is that I didn't really have any big insights, but I did meet some wonderful people and discovered that I can still enjoy travelling alone. Before leaving home I was a little scared at the idea, but my short Camino gave me more confidence to do something without being in a relationship and confirmed my decision. It was a very interesting experience and I have decided to travel alone more often. But I think the Camino gave me even more than that, though I can't quite define what it is, at least not yet. I'll let you know when it's clearer in my mind.

And what of Marina and Gabriella...? There must be a reason that you're always surrounded by women ;) I look forward to hearing more about your Camino and what it brings you.

Wade, I really do wish you much love, and tenderness.

Big hug

love

Angelina x

He was so happy and full of emotion to hear from her and he tried to send a reply right away. But the computer was impossibly slow and kept crashing before he had finished writing, and when he did press 'send' he saw that the message appeared to be empty. Eventually, he had to give up and send a text on his mobile phone instead:

I got your email tonight. Ran out of time before I could reply fully, so please excuse the abrupt ending. Wish you were with me now. Love Wade x

Back in his room at the Hostal Santa Maria, Wade reflected on his feelings for this young woman – this angel. On the one hand, though she was far too young for him, her email had lifted his hopes again. On the other hand, he remembered his grandfather's words of wisdom: "There's no fool like an old fool." He took pen and notepad and composed a short verse:

Can you live without love?

Yes, I have for many years.

Have you missed anything?

Much joy and many tears.

Is that the way you want it?

No, it's not the way to go.

In spite of the comfortable bed and warm room, Wade had a restless night. When he did get to sleep he was disturbed by strange and vivid dreams of deformed children wearing dirty shirts, and an elusive young woman that he was trying to catch. But which one? Was it Angelina, Gabriella, or someone else?

*

After breakfast at El Molino, Wade set out in the wintry sunshine. The temperature was barely above freezing, so he walked briskly to keep warm. There was little traffic and Wade followed the main road route towards Villafranca del Bierzo. After a time he saw another walker, a woman with a backpack in the distance some way in front, and then just ahead of him he noticed a jacket lying on the ground. He picked it up and waving the jacket in the air called out to the woman ahead. She turned around, waved back and waited for Wade to catch up. He gave her the jacket.

"Hi, thanks a lot, I guess I didn't tie it on properly," she said with a smile.

Her name was Emma, and she was a sturdy young Australian woman in her mid-thirties. She liked to chat and this suited Wade, who was glad of some company after the solitude of the previous day, but he was sorry to hear she would only be walking as far as the next town.

"Today's walk is just a warm up really," she told him. "I wanted to get a taste of what it's like to walk alone before I meet up with some friends in Sarria tomorrow. We're going to walk the last 100 kilometres of the Camino together, so I'll be taking a bus to Sarria when we get to Villafranca."

By the time they arrived in Villafranca it was warm enough for them to sit outside in the sunshine to enjoy a coffee before Emma's bus arrived. Then Wade continued on his way, alone again, though he didn't feel the conflict of emotions that he had endured during his solitary walk the day before. In fact, he didn't feel anything much at all. It was one of those days when he just walked, following the yellow arrows, barely glancing at the scenery, each step bringing him closer to Santiago.

A couple of hours brisk walk brought him to Trabadelo. He had met nobody since leaving Emma in Villafranca, but here at a roadside bar, with tables outside in the sunshine, there was quite a gathering of young pilgrims, most of whom he already knew.

At one table the two Sebastians from Germany were playing guitar. With them was the young Argentinian, Enrique, while at a neighbouring table Texas Luke was sitting with another young man of about thirty.

"Hi Wade," said Luke. "Good to see you again. This is Nathan, from Canada. He's been walking for months, all over Europe."

They shook hands. It occurred to Wade that this was the second Nathan from Canada that he had met on the Camino.

"Where did you start today, Wade?" Luke asked.

Wade thought for a few seconds. He had just walked really, without thinking, and for the moment he wasn't quite sure where he had begun the day.

"I really can't think of the name just now," he said.

"Where are you aiming for tonight?"

"I'm not sure of that either," said Wade.

Nathan laughed. "Wow! You're a real peregrino," he said. "The only thing that matters is the ultimate goal – Santiago de Compostela."

Wade smiled and they shook hands again.

The others were ready to leave, but Wade stayed a little longer at the bar to drink another refreshing beer in the sunshine.

"We're all going as far as Vega de Valcarce," said Luke as he donned his backpack. "The municipal albergue in Vega is open all the year round. Hope to see you there."

The road to Vega was an easy walk. The pleasant views across the river valley were spoiled a little by the A6 motorway in the background, but this didn't concern Wade, who was only interested in progressing along the way. The albergue was just off the main village street, on his right-hand side and at first sight, it didn't look very inviting. The building was being renovated and the whole of the ground floor was a construction site, with just the first floor available for pilgrims. He thought about going on to try and find something better, but the group of young pilgrims he had met at the bar in Trabadelo hailed him from the open balcony on the first floor. He waved back and climbed up the stairs to join them.

The accommodation was basic. There were three rooms, each with the usual bunk beds, but no heating save for a small, portable, electric blower heater in the main room. There was a shower available, but no hot water. Simple cooking facilities and a table and chairs were situated on the open landing at the top of the stairs leading directly onto the balcony.

What am I doing here? thought Wade. But at least he would have some lively company and the friendly hospitalera gave him two extra blankets for his bunk.

It would be different.

They decided to cook for themselves. Wade would have preferred the restaurant he had noticed in the main street, but it was clear that some of the young guys were on a tight budget and he felt he should share the experience with them. He and Luke did some shopping in the village and brought back the makings of a simple meal – wine, bread, ingredients for a thick soup, cheese and tomatoes. Nathan volunteered to be the cook.

In the meantime, a few more pilgrims had arrived: a young Australian couple and a Canadian man. Wade looked around him. He was at least thirty years older than anyone else present.

Nathan, busy in the improvised kitchen, was having to discourage a family of hungry cats that kept trying to leap up onto the table where he was preparing the food.

"Can I give you a hand?" Wade asked.

"It's okay except for one slight problem."

"What's that?"

"Well, soup's on the menu but we don't seem to have enough spoons for all of us."

"I'll see if I can get some from the hospitalera."

When he returned with the spoons, he saw that everything was almost ready and the pilgrims had moved the table and chairs into the main room. Outside on the balcony and in the kitchen area, the temperature was well below freezing now, but with the portable heater and the balcony door closed they were just about warm enough.

Their simple meal became a feast, the conversation around the table was animated and there was much laughter. Wade, very much the grandfather of the party, was content just to listen for much of the time and enjoy witnessing the exuberance of youth.

When they had finished eating, they began making music. The two Sebastians played guitar well and sang in harmony. The younger of the two, who was slender and fair-haired, sang a catchy song he had written about the Camino.

"You could sell that song," someone said.

"Nobody is going to make any money from my Camino song," said Sebastian with some feeling. "It is special just for me. When the Camino is over, I will burn the song and give it to God."

Others took turns to sing or play the guitars and when they started to play the blues, Wade joined in. He felt he could sing the blues, he had done it decades before when as a young man he had spent that memorable summer on the beaches of Greece, chasing the girls, drinking and singing in the bars, falling in love with his future wife.

While the two Sebastians accompanied him on guitar, Wade sang:

It was on the Camino
I met a real nice girl.
It was on the Camino
I met a real nice girl.
She had the smile of an angel

And put my heart in a whirl.

We walked the way together

As far as León town.

We walked the way together

As far as León town.

But there she met another

And then she put me down.

Now I'm on my own again

Till I don't know when.

Now I'm on my own again

Till I don't know when

But although I'm alone now,

I'd do it over again.

Wade realised he had borrowed some of the text from his poem to Angelina, but it was difficult to invent a completely new rhyme as he went along. How had the old blues singers done it? It was practice, he supposed. In any case, it seemed to Wade that this was pretty basic stuff, but his young companions were kind pilgrims and applauded politely.

It was late when they all drifted off to bed and outside it was bitter cold. But who would have the only electric heater? By leaving the doors open to the three bunk rooms, with the heater near the doorways, each room had the benefit of a little heat. Even so, Wade was glad of his extra blankets. He wondered where the others had stopped for the night and sent a text to Marina:

Tonight in vegas. Feel good. W x

*

In the biting cold of the early morning, with the ground covered in white frost, Wade left the albergue with Enrique and they stopped at the first bar in the village for breakfast. Wade checked his mobile. Marina had replied to last night's text:

Lucky you!!! We are in villafranca de bierzo...Worse than in any place we were before...awful! I am a penguin now. See you! Buen camino!

So the others were some way behind him. But who did Marina mean by 'we'? He wondered if Gabriella had joined them.

When Wade and his companion set off again, they walked briskly to keep warm.

"Look!" said Enrique, pointing at the blue sky. "Over there you can still see the moon. When you can see the sun and moon at the same time in a blue sky, it's a good sign."

They walked together for a while, following the old road up the river valley, but the way was always uphill and it was a long climb to O'Cebreiro. Wade, who was not a great climber, was struggling to keep pace with his young companion.

"Enrique, don't feel you have to wait for me," he said. "It's better for me to go at my own pace. We'll meet again later on maybe."

"Okay! Then, adiós Wade and buen Camino!"

They shook hands and parted.

Wade found the steep climb up the final stretch to

O'Cebreiro quite demanding, though wonderful views across the river valley below kept his spirits high. Entering the village, he passed by the famous Camino church of Santa Maria la Real, but his thoughts were concentrated on arriving and finding a place to stay for the night. He would look at the church in the morning… maybe.

Wade's guidebook described how O'Cebreiro had once been deserted with little more than a few ruined buildings remaining from the original settlement. All this had changed in recent years and O'Cebreiro was now an established centre for tourists and pilgrims alike. Many of the original buildings had been restored, pensions, bars and restaurants established, and a smart new albergue had been built.

At the albergue, he was told that there was heating but no extra blankets available. The place looked really nice, but he decided not to risk being cold at night and went instead to a pension in the village with the luxury of a warm room, a comfortable bed and his own bathroom. Then later, after showering, he found a laundry in the village and while he waited for his clothes to be washed and dried, he returned to his room and sent a few texts, including one to Gabriella:

Tonight o'cebreiro. Single room w bath. Luxury! W x

A couple of minutes later he heard the familiar buzz of his mobile phone. It was a text from Gabriella.

Glad to know you r good. Same here. Quite disconnected and enjoying it. Cheers!

It certainly sounded like Gabriella was alone, didn't it? But where? He texted back:

And where are you, or is that a secret? In any case, i hope to see you in santiago. W x

Would the Camino have any more surprises for him, or had he learned all he was going to learn this time around?

He was feeling hungry by this time and got ready to go out to find somewhere to eat. It was icy cold outside, so after picking up his freshly washed clothes from the laundry, he quickly found a bar with a blazing fire in the hearth and sat at a table as near to it as he could. He ordered the peregrino menu and the food was plentiful and good, so was the wine, but he missed the company he had enjoyed at that simple albergue the previous night. Then a group of elderly Spanish men came in and stood at the bar, drinking wine and singing traditional songs. After a time one of them came over to Wade.

"You are peregrino?" he asked.

Wade smiled and nodded.

"We sing you old song," the man continued and beckoned to his companions to come over to the table where they formed a half circle in front of Wade.

Their song was a lively one, with a strangely haunting melody, sung in harmony and with passion. Wade noticed the word peregrino recurring frequently but could understand little else. Not for the first time did he wish that he could speak Spanish, and when they had finished each of them, in turn, shook his hand and wished him, "Buen Camino!" Wade felt himself fighting back the tears again.

When he got back to his room at the pension, he

noticed that he had received another text from Marina:

We are at albergue in o'cebreiro. Very comfortable. Really warm!

Was she referring to just Carlos and herself? Or was Philippe there too? Or even Gabriella?

*

That night Wade dreamed that he was walking by the sea, waves lapping gently on the sandy shore. Ahead of him at some distance, a young woman with blonde hair was walking too. No matter how hard he tried to catch her, she was always just out of reach. Who was she? Would he ever know? Finally, she turned around and stared at him and he saw that it was Sabina, looking just as she had done when he first knew her. Wade woke with a start, the image of the young woman still on his mind.

A few weeks after their brief holiday romance, Sabina had come from her home in Frankfurt to stay with Wade in London. He remembered the excitement of meeting her at Victoria Station, looking along the platform as passengers alighted from the boat train, seeing her at last, coming towards him, a young blonde girl with a huge suitcase. Nothing had changed, they were very much in love and they had spent the next two years in London, before deciding to make their home together in Germany. Why had they done that? Wade recalled that Sabina had accepted a place at university in Frankfurt, and he had happily given up his job – a temporary post at a tough school in East London.

"We can always come back if it doesn't work out,

Wade," she had told him.

It had never occurred to Wade that there might be difficulties. He had also never told Sabina about his Jewish grandmother. Maybe he should have.

Wade's room in O'Cebreiro was warm and comfortable, wooden shutters at the windows kept the room dark and it was quiet outside, so he didn't get up until well after seven o'clock. He felt refreshed and eager to walk on.

After he left the pension he went across the way to the bar opposite for breakfast. Marina, Carlos and Philippe were already there and with them was Dante, a tall, dark-haired, young Spaniard he hadn't met before. As they were having breakfast – the usual orange juice, coffee and a croissant – Marina quietly slipped a postcard into Wade's hand.

"For you," she said simply.

He looked at it, and instead of a picture there was a printed text in English entitled 'The Pilgrim's Prayer'. While the others were chatting he read it quickly and was immediately struck by its simple message, that even if you do everything that a good pilgrim should, it counts for nothing unless you find God. He put the postcard carefully away with his pilgrim passport.

"Thank you," he said to Marina and kissed her on the cheek.

The others were going to mass before continuing with their journey and although Wade thought about joining them, he really wanted to be alone to consider this new revelation. He decided to walk on.

Wade took his time. The way was mainly downhill and it was bitter cold at first. A white hoar frost coated the mountain slopes, while a thin mist rose mysteriously from the valleys. When he reached Alto San Roque, where there was a dramatic bronze statue of a medieval pilgrim leaning into the wind, he took off his backpack and stopped to admire the view across the mountains of Galicia. Taking out the postcard Marina had given him and reading 'The Pilgrim's Prayer' again, he felt a sense of abject failure. Had he achieved nothing during the past four weeks of walking the Camino?

"You are troubled?" said a voice at his shoulder. It was Diego, of course.

"Yes I am," said Wade somewhat bitterly. "I have a conflict of emotions. Even though I have learned to open my heart to a woman's love again, thanks to Angelina, I seem to have lost the way in the search for my God."

"But is it your heart you have opened, or is it a desire for sex with a young woman again before you die? Are you desperately trying to make up for all those lost years? Has it become a kind of 'bucket list' project in your mind?"

Wade shrugged his shoulders. "Maybe it is. It's becoming an obsession and getting in the way of my spiritual search I suppose."

"Of course it is," said Diego. "And you're not likely to achieve any success chasing after women half your age. It's pathetic. Be realistic and grow up."

Wade sighed. He knew Diego was right, but he couldn't help himself somehow. He looked westward across a palette of green and brown hills and valleys. Somewhere beyond those hills lay Santiago de Compostela, his physical goal. It was less than a week away now. He would continue his spiritual search when he got there and in the meantime, he would experience the thrill of the chase. He turned to speak to his friend and advisor again, but Diego had vanished.

Wade walked on, having put any thoughts of spiritual progress on hold for the time being, and he just enjoyed the scenery and the relatively easy walk down to Triacastela. He saw few other pilgrims along the way.

As he approached the village, he heard the familiar buzz of his mobile and eagerly checked the message. It was from Gabriella:

Me? Carpe diem! Buen camino!

Wade had not studied much Latin at school and had struggled with its conjugations and declinations from day one. Nevertheless, he felt that 'carpe diem' was an expression he should really know. He racked his brain, trying to remember. It was something like living for the moment, wasn't it? He decided to check it out later.

The municipal albergue was located on the outskirts of the village, set back some distance from the road and surrounded by open land. It was early afternoon and few, if any, pilgrims would have arrived yet. The place looked deserted and uninviting to Wade, who decided to walk on further into the village to find a private albergue.

At first glance, the rest of Tricastela looked deserted too, but eventually, he found what he was looking for – an albergue with heating, extra blankets and access to the internet. He checked in and found himself sharing a room with just one other person, a distinguished-looking, grey-haired Frenchman in his mid-sixties. They arranged to meet up later for dinner, but in the meantime, Wade was anxious to write his emails, in particular, one to Angelina. It seemed ages since he had been able to write to her. He went downstairs to use the albergue's computer.

Hi Angelina

I'm so happy you opened me up when you did. You taught me to open my heart again and that alone would make my Camino worthwhile. As I told you, I cried the next day in the Meseta and I've cried many times since, without really knowing why, but just filled with emotion. I've talked to a few people about this and others have had similar experiences. I think it has something to do with the fact that you are occupied with your mind, and alone for such long periods of time every day. It's not dissimilar to the silent retreat, which I remember telling you about, where the silence was too much for some retreatants to bear.

Now I'm only 6 days from Santiago (I expect to arrive on 30th November) and the third stage from Leon has taken on its own special identity. Again I've compared notes with others and they are having a similar experience. Many of us seem to be slowing down, perhaps because we don't want it to end. I don't know for sure. Last week, though, I just wanted to get to Santiago and go home. The emotions are slowing down too and the bursts of tears are seldom now.

I sort of believe in signs and I've been expecting three things to learn from this Camino. The first was from you, where you taught me to open my heart. The next lesson was a reminder of the pain that can come from opening my heart again when I tried out the new me on Gabriella. I believe I got an insight into the third event this morning. Marina gave me a text about the good pilgrim, who shares with others, tries to love everyone, helps where he/she can and so on. But the text ends with the thought that this is all for nothing if you have no God. I have 6 days to Santiago to reread and consider this. I've been to church quite a lot lately.

I think if you had gone further with the Camino you would have had more insights too. The confidence to be and to travel alone is worth a lot. I hadn't realised it was a problem for you till now. I don't suppose you will be alone for long unless it's what you want. You're a lovely woman and a beautiful person in every way. I'll always remember the short time I spent with you on Camino and I truly hope that we will meet again before long. I'll send some more texts along the way and write an email to you again when I get to Santiago. In the meantime, I will think of you often with love and affection, my sweet Angelina.

Wade x

He returned to his room after he had finished with the computer. His room-mate Pierre-André was already there, reading a book. He looked up when Wade came in.

"I don't know about you, but I'm already beginning to feel hungry," he said. "I've been looking around the village while you were writing your emails and I've found a small restaurant just down the street. They open at seven."

"Sounds good to me," said Wade, looking at his

watch. "There's just time for a short rest before we go."

The night was cold, with a clear sky full of twinkling stars, and the two men hurried to the little restaurant, where they were the first customers of the evening. They ordered a bottle of red wine before looking further at the menu. The kitchen staff had only just arrived so it would take some time for their meal to be ready.

They raised their glasses. "Salud! Buen Camino!"

"I hope you don't mind me saying this, but I've never met a Frenchman before who speaks such perfect English, just like a BBC newsreader," said Wade.

Pierre-André laughed. "I taught English and Latin at a private school for many years, I was also the headmaster." He paused for a moment before adding: "I have just recently retired."

Wade suddenly remembered the last text message he had received from Gabriella and asked Pierre-André about the exact meaning of 'carpe diem'.

"I suppose I should know this," said Wade apologetically, "but I'm really not sure. I think it's something about living for the moment, isn't it?"

"That's correct," said Pierre-André with a smile. " It's often translated into English as 'seize the day', but as a Latin scholar, I consider that 'enjoy the day' is more in the spirit of the original."

Wade was thoughtful. "But there's a slight difference in meaning between the two, isn't there?" he said. "Or at least there can be."

"Absolutely."

The two men ordered their meal, together with a second bottle of wine, and talked about their lives, as pilgrims do.

"Like you, I am divorced," said Pierre-André. "Unfortunately, it was a very expensive business for me and I've had to change my lifestyle. Also, of course, I have to live on a modest pension now."

The Frenchman paused for a few moments and gazed wistfully into his glass before continuing.

"When I had money, I used to own a yacht. She was my passion for many years. We even sailed across the Atlantic twice. It was a wonderful adventure, but I couldn't afford to keep my yacht any longer and eventually I had to sell her. It nearly broke my heart and I miss the adventure. That's why I'm doing the Camino now, I suppose."

Wade thought for a moment before replying. "Another pilgrim told me that most people come on the Camino for one of two reasons: either they have lost their job, or a relationship has come to an end. I think this applies to you and your yacht."

"Yes, of course," said his friend. "A boat is always 'she'. It was a very special relationship for me."

While they had been talking and eating a few more pilgrims had come into the restaurant, including a party of three attractive German girls. They appeared to know Pierre-André and greeted him before sitting at a table across the room.

"They're pretty girls," said Wade softly. "You know them?"

"Yes, we met at a municipal albergue some days

ago. You know, sometimes I wish I were thirty-five years younger."

"You too?" Wade replied. "It's a wish that I often have, and it's stopping me from making any sort of spiritual progress during my pilgrimage."

"You see the one in the centre?" said Pierre-André quietly, glancing briefly towards the German girls. "Well, in the middle of the night at the albergue, I had to get up to go to the toilet – the prostate, you know."

"I know the problem well," said Wade.

"There was only one bathroom on our floor at the albergue, with toilet cubicles and some washbasins. The only shower was downstairs. It was all a bit primitive. Anyway, I entered the bathroom and there she was, standing stark naked at a washbasin. She turned briefly to look at me – her body was beautiful – and then she continued washing herself, quite unconcerned with my presence. I didn't know where to look, but I still had to use the toilet. So I went into the cubicle, did what I had to do and then left the bathroom. As I left, I glanced across at her and she was still standing there at the washbasin, her youthful body glistening with soapy water. It's an image that I will not forget in a hurry."

"Wow!" said Wade. "And could you sleep after that?"

Pierre-André smiled wistfully. "What do you think?"

Back at the albergue, as Wade lay in bed thinking of Pierre-Andre's story, he remembered the beautiful German girl he had married all those years ago.

That first year in Frankfurt had been difficult: he didn't speak the language, he couldn't find a job. He had found German people arrogant and overbearing. He had begun to feel his Jewishness and he wanted to go back to London.

But Sabina, happy to be back in Frankfurt, had dug her heels in.

"Wade, this is my home, I like it here, and I'm not going back to live in England again. If you don't want to stay here, you can go, but you will go alone."

This had been their first real fight, but it had been a decisive one. Wade had thought long and hard about returning to London, but when Sabine became pregnant everything had changed. He knew he had to stay, even though it meant losing control of his own destiny.

*

Wade met up with his Camino friends for breakfast at a bar in Tricastela. They had spent the night at the municipal albergue and were planning to walk to Sarria via the route past the famous Benedictine monastery at Samos. It was a cold, clear, sunny day though the moon was still visible in the early morning sky when they set out. *A good sign,* thought Wade, remembering his conversation with Enrique a few days earlier.

Wade realised he had spent quite a lot of time walking alone recently and now he enjoyed the company of the others, chatting and joking as they followed the way. Unfortunately, the huge monastery was not open to visitors when they arrived in Samos, but they stopped in the village for a bite to eat anyway. Sitting outside in the sunshine they could see the imposing granite stone building across the valley and they joked about the unlikely possibility of Philippe becoming a monk.

Marina laughed. "Philippe, now that you've heard from Gabriella at last, I think you don't want to join the monastery anymore."

"Yes, but she's probably about two days behind us," Philippe replied with a rueful smile. "I think I won't see her before we get to Santiago."

All this was news to Wade. Philippe clearly had the advantage now. He felt he might have missed the opportune moment by not reacting to her mysterious 'Carpe diem!' message. What if she had meant that he should seize the moment and go for it? He would probably never know.

Dante, who was still new to the group, asked Wade how he was coping with the Camino.

Wade thought for a moment before replying.

"It's no great problem physically. The difficulties lie in the heart and in the mind."

Philippe looked at him closely. "I think so too," he said.

Wade wondered if Gabriella would turn up in Santiago with more members of the fan club – Richard for example. He sensed that Philippe wasn't so sure of his chances either. Gabriella appeared to enjoy stringing her men along.

It didn't bother him greatly, because Angelina was the woman who really meant something to him. He hoped that he hadn't overdone things with his most recent email to her. He decided to send her a text:

Hi Angelina, i do hope my last email wasn't too emotional. Please excuse me if it was. Now on the way to sarria. Love Wade x

They continued as a group to Sarria, a small town with many albergues. Here they could expect a new influx of pilgrims because to earn a Compostela it was necessary to walk at least the final hundred kilometres to Santiago, and Sarria was the last station before the hundred-kilometre waymark. For many pilgrims, this would be the start of their short Camino. Wade wondered who would choose to start their pilgrimage at the end of November.

The albergue was warm and comfortable, with plenty of blankets for the beds, and it had a kitchen too. They decided to eat in, with Carlos and Marina in charge of the cooking as usual, and as they sat around the table eating their evening meal they talked about their plans for the remainder of the Camino.

"It's normally four days' walk from here," said Carlos, who had done the Camino before. "You can do it in three days, but then you arrive in Santiago in the late afternoon. It's better to arrive earlier so that you have plenty of time to collect your Compostela, visit the cathedral, maybe have a late lunch and generally celebrate what you've achieved."

"To enjoy the day," said Wade, thoughtfully.

Carlos smiled. "Exactly."

"I've read that there's a special mass every day at noon," said Marina. "I really want to go to that and also to see the famous Botafumeiro in action."

"Botafumeiro? What's that?" Wade asked.

"It's a huge incense burner, suspended from the ceiling. Some monks pull on the rope and the Botafumeiro swings from side to side above the people. It goes very high and nearly touches the ceiling."

"I want to see that too," said Philippe.

*

Wade had noticed that he urgently needed some more money, so he went to look for a cash machine early the next morning. There were no banks open at this time of day and it took him quite a while to find a cashpoint. Then when he inserted his euro cashcard, it was rejected by the machine – the account was empty. He would have to use his UK debit card from now on. By the time he eventually managed to complete his transaction and find his way back to the albergue, his friends had already left.

The marked route led through quiet lanes and pathways and he saw few other pilgrims. His plan was to spend the night in Portomarín, where he would probably meet up with the others, and he walked on steadily, automatically, paying little attention to the scenery, though one corner of his brain was always switched on to note the waymarks and yellow arrows ahead.

When he eventually stopped for lunch, he checked his mobile for messages. His heart leapt with excitement: there was a text from Angelina:

Hi Wade, it was a beautiful email, not too emotional at all. Can't go to mallorca now. On top of that, I'm in bed with a (light) concussion. Enjoy your last kilometres. Once you finish, you'll miss it. Big hug x

Wow! She thought his email was beautiful. He needn't have worried about it after all. But what was this about having concussion? He replied right away:

How did you get concussion? Are you sure you're ok? Love Wade

The reply came just a few minutes later:

I'm ok, but very bored. Tried to work today but had to go home at noon with a headache. Just a little accident. I fell and hurt my head. No big deal. Only wait and sleep. Soon you'll be in santiago. Mixed feelings I guess. Will you walk on to finistere?

He texted back, before continuing on his way:

Expect to arrive in santiago on saturday. Not sure what my feelings will be, but certain to be intense. Maybe some others from our burgos family will be there. I hope so. Don't know about finistere yet. Take care. Will text again tomorrow. Love wade

He kissed the screen of his mobile when he sent the message. He really did love that young woman, even though he hardly knew her. It was crazy. He couldn't see a happy ending, though he longed for her.

He walked steadily on and eventually reached the approach to Portomarín, which was over a long, high, modern bridge spanning the River Miño far below. To Wade, who had no great head for heights, it really did look a long way down to the river. The road over the bridge was bordered by a narrow footway, with just low metal railings between him and the abyss below. He felt insecure and crossed cautiously, stooping, his eyes fixed on the footway just a few metres ahead of him, trying to avoid looking over the railings on his right. He hoped no one was watching.

Wade's first impression of Portomarín, like so many small towns and villages along the way, was that it had closed down for the winter. He strolled through the deserted streets looking for signs of an albergue. Why didn't he just look for an address in his guidebook? He didn't know really. These days he just trusted to fate that he would find a place for the night. Something would turn up – it always did.

He spotted a small albergue in a side street, with the entrance door wide open and the hospitalera sitting in reception, awaiting customers. It was cold in reception and he asked about heating and blankets in his pidgin Spanish before making up his mind whether to stay or not:

"Aquí calefacción y mantas?"

The hospitalera showed him the small dormitory with radiators and blankets and he checked in. There was no one else in the room at first, but he noticed that two other bunks were already taken.

Wade decided to get cleaned up and when he returned from the showers, his room-mates had just come back from the supermarket. They were a couple in their late fifties – Rachel from Alaska and Nils from Denmark. They were clearly travelling together, but Wade had a feeling that they hadn't known each other very long.

"Look, we've bought far too much stuff at the supermarket," said Rachel. "Would you like to have dinner with us? There's a kitchen we can use just along the corridor."

"Rachel's a good cook," said Nils, patting his ample stomach.

Wade gratefully accepted the invitation before going out to the nearby supermarket to buy a bottle of wine, as his contribution to the feast, and when he returned Rachel was in the middle of conjuring up a huge stir fry in the kitchen.

The meal was delicious and when Rachel got ready to wash up afterwards, Wade intervened. "No, please, you've done more than enough. I'll do the washing up later when we've finished the wine."

It was lovely and warm in the kitchen and the three pilgrims sat together around the table chatting for a while about the Camino. Nils and Rachel had both started in St-Jean, but it wasn't until Burgos that they had met and continued the way together. In due course, Nils produced a second bottle, but Rachel retired to her bunk soon afterwards, leaving the two men to drink the wine.

"Rachel doesn't drink much," said Nils.

They were silent for a while, and then he added: "I'm so glad I met her. It's made all the difference to my Camino. We're both divorced and Rachel's good company and... well, we enjoy the sex now and again. But not tonight," he added with a laugh.

"I'm divorced too," said Wade, "but I seem condemned to walk alone."

"Haven't you met anyone you fancied on the Camino?"

"Yes I have, actually, and I fell in love in Burgos. At least I think so."

"So what happened to the woman?"

"That's where she finished her Camino and had to

fly back home."

"Did she feel the same way about you?"

"I'm not sure, but sometimes I like to think so. The big problem is our age difference."

Nils looked at him. "Ah, so is she much younger than you?"

"She's young enough to be my daughter."

"And how old are you?"

"Sixty-nine."

"Really! You don't look it. And the woman?"

"Thirty-three I think."

"Wow! You're certainly ambitious. But think about it in practical terms, Wade. Even if she loves you too, how long can it last? A few years maybe, if you're very lucky, by which time you'll be an old man and she'll still be a relatively young woman. I can't see it ever working," said Nils. "Look, Wade, the Camino plays tricks on your mind and you think you're young again, but if you're honest with yourself, you'll know you are far too old for her."

He finished his glass of wine and stood up. "Goodnight Wade. I think you said you'd do the washing up."

"Goodnight!"

While he was washing the dishes Wade thought over what Nils had said. He was right, of course.

*

Now, in late November, Portomarín seemed to be in hibernation. When Wade left the albergue the next morning, looking for somewhere to have breakfast, he could only find one café open. There were just a few pilgrims inside and he saw Carlos, Marina and Philippe sitting together at a corner table. He ordered coffee and a croissant and went over to join his friends.

Philippe was preoccupied with his mobile.

"He's had a message from Gabriella," said Marina. "And he's trying to work out where she is."

"I think she cannot be more than two days behind us," said Philippe. "I will try to find out before I move on from Portomarín."

Gabriella was clearly the focus of Philippe's Camino now. She had become his obsession.

Just as they were getting ready to leave, some more pilgrims came in and among them, Wade noticed a familiar face. It was Katrine, the young Danish woman he had met briefly at the albergue in Astorga. She appeared to see him too. He nodded in her direction and smiled.

While Philippe stayed in Portomarín, Wade walked on with Carlos and Marina. There was the usual blue sky and sunshine that Wade had come to expect.

"It is not normal for Galicia at this time of year," Carlos told him. "It usually rains almost as much as in your country."

"God is being kind to us," said Marina with a smile.

"And another thing," said Carlos. "Because of all this sunshine, I can tell that you have walked the Camino de Santiago just by looking at you."

"How do you mean?" said Wade.

"Just look at your hands. The back of the left hand is much browner than the right one. We are always walking in the same direction – east to west – and so the sun is always coming from our left side."

Wade checked his hands. "You're right," he said. "But it doesn't work with you, Carlos."

Carlos laughed. "With my dark skin, you can see that the sun must be always shining in my heart."

When they reached the small town of Palas de Rei, their aim for the day, the dusk was descending. While Carlos and Marina took a double room at a pension near the town centre, Wade checked in at the private albergue across the road, which had a bar in reception.

"We can see you here for breakfast," said Marina. "Philippe may arrive later. He sent me a text to say he would not wait in Portomarín after all."

Wade found himself sharing a room on the second floor with just one other pilgrim and after taking a shower and getting changed he returned to the bar on the ground floor for a beer. The only other customer at the time was a young woman sitting alone at a corner table. It was Katrine again, so Wade went over to speak to her.

"May I join you?"

"Yes, of course."

"Can I buy you another beer?"

"No thanks, this one is enough for me."

"When did you arrive?"

"About ten minutes ago." Katrine nodded towards her backpack, which was propped up against the wall.

"I haven't been to my room yet. The hospitalero is going to take me there in a few minutes. He says I am lucky. It is a room just for women and so far I am the only one."

The hospitalero suddenly appeared from behind the bar and came over to their table.

"Please come with me and I'll take you to your room now. It's on the second floor, so we will take the elevator. By the way, we have a small restaurant down in the basement. It opens at seven o'clock if you would like to have dinner. This is a very small town and I think you will not find anywhere else."

"Do you have a peregrino menu?" Wade asked.

"Yes, of course, and not expensive."

Before Katrine went to her room, she and Wade arranged to meet in the restaurant later, shortly after seven.

For the moment, Wade sat at the table finishing his beer and considering what his chances were with this new young woman. She wasn't very tall, but quite sporty looking, with a pretty face, fair hair, probably in her late thirties. And she seemed to be travelling alone now – that was good to know. He took a last swig of his beer. Why was he thinking like this? He obviously hadn't learned his lesson yet.

A few minutes after seven he went down to the tiny restaurant in the basement. Katrine was already there and he joined her at a small table directly opposite the kitchen. For the moment, they were the only customers.

"I'm very hungry," Katrine said. "I've hardly eaten

all day, so I'm really ready for this. But it will take a while because the cook has only just arrived."

They ordered a bottle of wine while they were waiting for the meal.

"When I saw you in Astorga, you were travelling with some French guys," said Wade. "What happened to them?"

"They were too slow for me, so eventually I went on ahead. I've been travelling alone for a couple of days now."

As they waited for the meal, they talked about their respective Caminos.

"I'm really looking forward to Santiago now," said Wade. "Just three more days. It's hard to believe."

"I'm in a bit of a dilemma," Katrine replied, "and I may try to do it in two days."

"Why's that?"

"My flight back to Denmark is booked for a week today, but I would like to walk on to Finistere if I can. I think this is just possible if I walk fast and don't hang around in Santiago." She took a sip of her wine. "But I haven't quite made up my mind yet."

While they were talking, a rather large, middle-aged man had entered the restaurant and sat down at the next table. He was not only tall, but also quite obese, and when he spoke, it was clear from his accent that he came from the southern states of the USA. He questioned the waitress about the menu in a loud voice, before ordering what seemed to Wade to be a vast amount of food. He then interrupted Wade and Katrine's conversation to introduce himself before preaching a monologue about his Camino. He told them he was representing his church in Alabama, where he was the Pastor, and how he was sending his congregation regular reports. Apparently, he was also writing a book about the Camino, recording the experiences of the people he met along the way. He began to cross-examine Katrine:

"Now tell me, just why are you doing this Camino? I'm sure you have a special reason."

Katrine clearly didn't like the question. "It's very personal. I'm certainly not telling someone I've just met my reasons for walking the Camino."

The Alabama Preacher (as Wade had christened him in his mind) seemed quite unconcerned about her answer and would have continued with his questions except for the arrival of three other fat men, but somewhat younger, who were clearly part of his entourage. They were all friendly enough, but there was something about them that Wade found disturbing.

"They have bad vibes," Katrine whispered to him. "Let's go!"

Wade and Katrine paid their bill and went upstairs to the bar for a nightcap. While they were there, who should come into the bar from the street than the two Sebastians, the German boys, with their guitars.

"Hola! Are you staying here too?" Wade asked them.

"No, we are staying at the municipal albergue down the street," said the fair-haired Sebastian. "It's simple, but okay. Actually, we're looking for some American guys we met yesterday. We spent the evening drinking with them and they paid for everything. They said they would be here tonight. Have you seen them?"

"Yes, you'll find them in the restaurant downstairs in the basement."

"Great! Buen Camino!"

"Buen Camino, but take care!"

The boys left and Wade looked thoughtful. "I wonder if there's an ulterior motive," he said.

"Of course," said Katrine. "It's the free drinks that are the motive."

"It wasn't the boys' motive that I meant," Wade replied.

*

They had arranged to meet in the bar for breakfast very early the next morning. Wade would normally have made a much later start, but he wanted to try his luck with this young woman. He was sitting on a bar stool at the counter, drinking coffee, when Katrine arrived. She sat on the neighbouring stool, but he noticed she moved it slightly further away from his before she sat down.

"Did you sleep all right?" he asked.

"No, not very well. Didn't you hear the noise that those drunken Amis made in the middle of the night?"

"You mean the Alabama Preacher and his followers?"

"Yes, of course."

"Yes, I heard them. I'm only glad that I didn't have to share a room with them."

When they left the albergue it was very cold

outside. The sky was dark, clear and full of stars and they had to walk briskly to keep warm. Much of the way followed woodland paths and crossed several small rivers and they saw nobody for a couple of hours. Neither of them said much. Katrine seemed to be wrapped up in her own thoughts and Wade was reluctant to disturb her.

Not until they stopped for coffee at a small bar along the way did Katrine become more talkative. She was an unemployed teacher and somewhat bitter about it.

"I was having to work as a supply teacher," she said. "I got this position at a school where the regular teacher was on maternity leave and I took over her class. It was great fun and the kids really liked me, but when the original teacher returned I had to leave. It's not fair. I'm a good teacher."

"And your plan now?"

"I have to get back to Denmark as soon as possible to be available for work, otherwise I will lose my unemployment benefit."

"Maybe you should forget about going on to Finistere," said Wade. "You don't want to risk missing your flight back to Denmark next week."

"I've been thinking about that all morning so far," said Katrine, "but I'm fit, I can walk fast and I like the challenge. I know I can do it."

As they finished their coffee in silence, Wade recalled his own time as a supply teacher, at that tough school in East London. Unlike Katrine, he had not enjoyed the experience. In fact, he had hated every second of it, but he had been unable to get a permanent post after the Amy affair.

When they reached Melide they stopped for lunch at a busy bar located on the way into town. Many people were eating pulpo (octopus), a Galician speciality, but both Wade and Katrine opted for more familiar dishes. They were joined a few minutes later by the tall Dante and a Japanese pilgrim he had been walking with.

"Hola!" said Dante. "Why aren't you eating pulpo? You should try it. It's famous here."

Wade smiled. "Another time maybe, but I'm happy with pork today."

Dante and Wade chatted, but Katrine had little to say. She had withdrawn again into her own world and before long called the waiter over to pay her bill.

Wade was uncertain what to do.

"It's okay," said Dante with a grin. "I'll see you later."

Wade hurriedly paid and joined Katrine outside in the street.

"I'm sorry," she said. "I was not in the mood for socialising. I just had to get moving somehow."

They walked on briskly and Wade had to work hard to keep up. He began to suspect she was trying to get rid of him. Then, quite abruptly, she slowed down, dropping ever further behind, and clearly was hoping that he would walk on ahead.

Wade continued alone. The sun was shining, but inside he felt dejected, or should it be rejected? He stopped for a rest on a grassy patch at the side of the track and after some time Katrine came strolling by.

She greeted him with a smile but didn't stop, and a few minutes later Wade continued on his way in a black mood. Many pilgrims had described the Camino as being a rollercoaster, with its sudden highs and lows, and Wade had plunged to the depths. Here he was, completely alone, just a couple of days short of Santiago and what had the Camino given him? Nothing good that he could think of.

He continued in this black mood until Arzúa, where he saw Katrine some way ahead of him. He caught her up and joined her when she stopped at a bar for a coffee. She was friendly enough, without being effusive, and they walked on together to look for an albergue.

Arzúa, a popular stop on the Camino route during the warmer months, was like a ghost town. Hardly anything was open, but they eventually found an albergue at the far end of the town. It wasn't very special, but it had the basic facilities. Though heating was minimal, just a single convector heater in the middle of a large dormitory, the bunks had enough blankets. Among the other pilgrims there were some familiar faces, but no sign of Marina, Carlos or Philippe. Katrine chose a bunk right in a corner of the dormitory and Wade took the one next to her. Once he had showered and changed, he decided to send Marina a text:

Tonight, albergue los caminantes in arzua. And you? W x

A couple of minutes later, he received a reply. Marina and the others were in Arzúa too, but staying at another place nearby, and they arranged to meet for dinner later at a small restaurant, just around the corner.

In the meantime, Wade wanted to send an email to Angelina. There was a computer in the reception at the albergue and when he went online he found a message from Danilo in his inbox:

Hi Wade!

Always great to have news from you! Maja and I will walk tomorrow to Santiago! We have just the last 20km ! We can not believe it!!

I know you met Emma from Australia! We met her near Palas de Rei! Was very funny because when I start to talk about you she says she knows you!! Jaja! That is the Camino!!!

I don't know how long we stay in Santiago! We keep in contact. Look forward to see you soon!

The best to you!!!

A big hug from Maja!!

Adiós!

The email had been written two days before, so Danilo and Maja would probably have left Santiago before Wade's arrival. He decided to reply later, as the computer was incredibly slow and the reception area was rather chilly and uninviting. Even so, he just had to send a message to Angelina:

Hi Angelina

I'll tell you all about the Gabriella story when I get back to the UK, on my own computer and not in some useless internet cafe where nothing works properly and time runs out before I can finish. Have you ever seen a French farce at the theatre? It was a bit like that really.

Same with the insights, I can't go into that just now- maybe I'll have more chance in Santiago, where I plan to spend a few days. These things always come in threes :)

But more important than all this stuff is the situation with your concussion. I've sent a couple of text messages, yesterday and today, hoping to hear from you about it, but no news at all, and I'm sad and worried. How are you? Do let me know please with a short text.

Don't know if I'll walk to Finistere after all. Feeling a bit low just now and just want to finish the Camino and fly home.

Do let me know how you are. Take care.

Lots of love.

Wade x

Before shutting down the computer he had a quick look through his inbox to see if there were any other new messages of any interest. As he did so, he noticed that the email from his solicitor, concerning the mysterious Eve Dawson, was missing. That was strange. Somewhere along the line, when he was clearing out unwanted emails, he must have accidentally deleted it. Now he would never know what she had to say about Amy, but maybe that was for the best,

Minutes later, Wade and Katrine were hurrying through the chilly night air to the restaurant, where they were to meet the others. The five pilgrims were the only customers there, but they were greeted by a friendly waitress who turned out to be the cook for the evening too. After pushing two small tables together to form one long rectangular table surface, Katrine and Marina sat down on one side, with Carlos between them, while Wade and Philippe sat on the opposite side.

The menu was simple and the service was slow, but they talked and drank red wine while they were waiting. The atmosphere of the gathering was low key. Wade was feeling somewhat depressed, Katrine was moodily occupied with her smartphone, Marina and Philippe didn't have much to say either. Carlos was the only one making any effort to liven up the party. He picked up his smartphone, which was lying on the table in front of him, and turned towards Katrine on his left.

"Can I add you to my Facebook friends?" he asked her with a winning smile.

She agreed and gave him her contact details.

"Now, can I just have a picture for my address book? Smile, please!"

Katrine put on a wan smile for the photo, which Wade considered was more than she had managed for the whole evening till now.

Both Carlos and Katrine were now tapping away on their smartphones. Wade thought it very odd to ask someone you'd just met, and hardly knew, to become your Facebook friend.

At times like this, he realised that he belonged to an earlier generation. Though he had a Facebook account himself, he had rarely used it before the Camino. What's more, he didn't have a smartphone, just an ordinary mobile, which he used principally for sending text messages.

They all left the restaurant soon after finishing the meal. It hadn't been a very happy evening somehow, at least that's what Wade felt about it. Once they got outside, Katrine didn't even wait for him to finish saying goodnight to the others but hurried on ahead to the albergue.

Now it was late evening and the rest of the inmates had gone to bed. The dormitory was cold and dark, only lit up by the red button of the tiny portable heater in the centre of the room. They went to their bunks without a word. Katrine had even rigged up her bath towel to act as a kind of screen and discourage any communication. Wade mumbled, "Goodnight!" but there was no answer.

*

He woke up when Katrine's alarm went off in the early morning. It was pitch dark and the air was cold. Katrine moved around quietly, packing her gear by the light of a torch, and after a few minutes, she left without a word.

Wade stayed in bed a while longer, but he couldn't go back to sleep. He was in low spirits. His Camino adventure was fizzing out like a damp squib. Here he was, just two days' walk from Santiago, and what had he achieved? Virtually nothing! His attempts to find a woman had been a disaster and, more importantly, he had failed to find his God.

When the lights came on, Wade got up, dressed and quickly got ready to leave.

Outside, the ground was white with frost, though a pale sun was climbing in the sky. He would have loved a coffee, but there was nowhere open on the way out of town, so he walked on hoping to find a café or a bar in one the villages along the way.

He saw nobody at all for the first few kilometres, then after about an hour, he spotted another pilgrim on the track some way ahead. From the silhouette and the pink anorak, he guessed it could be Marina, and when he caught her up a few minutes later he saw that she had been crying.

"Hola Marina. Are you okay?"

"No, it's not good."

She didn't offer any explanation or say anything more for a few moments.

"You are not with your friend today?" she said eventually.

"Katrine? No, she's in a hurry," said Wade. "She wants to make Santiago today, so she left very early this morning, about six-thirty."

Marina's expression changed as if she had suddenly realised something. At the same time, the penny dropped with Wade too. He hesitated before speaking again.

"Look, would you like some company, or do you prefer to be alone right now?"

"Thank you. I want to be alone at the moment."

"Okay, I'll go on ahead. See you later for lunch maybe?"

She gave him a pale smile. "Yes, in Salceda there is a bar, Casa Verde, which my guidebook says is sure to be open. Send me a text and I will meet you there."

Wade walked briskly on. Now it was clear what had happened. Now he understood why Carlos had been so interested in getting Katrine's Facebook contact details. He had clearly arranged a rendezvous and had probably done this while they were all having dinner together the previous evening. That's what all the tapping away on their smartphones had been about.

When he got to the Casa Verde, situated directly at the roadside on the Camino route, he ordered a beer and sent Marina a text right away. While he was waiting for her to arrive, he looked around at the room. He was the only customer at the moment, but it was clear from the various shirts and other souvenirs hanging on the walls and ceiling that this was a popular stopping place for pilgrims.

By the time Marina got there, she appeared to have recovered her composure. Wade waited for her to broach the subject of Carlos's disappearance, but she didn't do so. Instead, they discussed their goal for the day, O Pedrouzo, while lunching on bocadillos and beer.

They had just left the bar and were standing in the road outside when they were hailed by an approaching pilgrim.

"Hola! Hola! Good to see you." It was Ayumi, the tiny Japanese lady Wade had met just after leaving Burgos, and she was walking merrily along at a lively pace.

The three of them continued on the way together, and gradually Marina began to cheer up a bit.

"If there is a kitchen at the albergue tonight, maybe we can cook something together," she suggested.

They were still talking about what they might eat that evening when they were approached by a young man who was handing out leaflets.

"There is a new albergue in O Pino," he told them. "It only opened recently. It is very fine and has everything you need."

"Does it have a kitchen?" Marina asked.

"Yes, of course. Kitchen, laundry, hot showers, everything. Everything is new."

They examined the leaflet – the albergue Cruceiro de Pedrouzo, with all its facilities, certainly looked attractive. It was just off the main Camino route, but there was a map with the leaflet and it should be easy to find. After a short discussion, they decided to go there.

On arrival, they entered a large open-plan area on the ground floor, with lounge, dining and kitchen space all for the use of pilgrims. As advertised, everything was new.

"The dormitory and other facilities are downstairs," the young lady at the front desk told them.

Wade was the first to check in and went downstairs ahead of Marina and Ayumi, who had gone to look at the kitchen facilities first. He descended the staircase down to the vast dormitory, where so far only a few bunks had been taken. Then, much to his surprise, he saw the familiar figure of Carlos, standing near the foot of the stairs.

Carlos, looking slightly embarrassed, greeted him.

"Hola, Wade."

"Carlos, I didn't expect to see you here. Are you alone?"

"No, see those bunks in the corner? Philippe is over there."

"It wasn't Philippe that I meant. Is Katrine here too?"

Carlos, looking at the floor, shook his head.

"Good!" said Wade. "Because Marina's here."

Wade dumped his backpack on a vacant bunk and went back upstairs, where the two women were still looking around the kitchen area.

"There's someone you know down there," he said to Marina.

She gave him a puzzled look before picking up her bag and making her way to the staircase.

Wade thought it best to keep out of the way for the time being. "Let's have a beer before we do anything else," he said to Ayumi with a smile.

By the time he eventually went down to the dormitory again, many more pilgrims had arrived. It looked like the place would be fairly full that evening. He noticed that Marina and Carlos, who were sitting hand in hand on the edge of a bunk in the corner of the vast room and talking earnestly together, seemed to be resolving their differences.

Wade unpacked his gear and went to the showers. It was very busy in there and he had to wait for one to be free. He had just finished and was on his way back to the dormitory when met Carlos.

"Everything okay now?"

Carlos nodded. "Yes, we've sorted things out."

"That was a clever trick you and Katrine played

with Facebook," said Wade rather mischievously.

Carlos lowered his eyes, looking suitably repentant, and Wade felt sorry that he had mentioned it.

"Katrine walks very fast," said Carlos at last.

"Well, you knew she wanted to get as far as Santiago today."

Back in the dormitory, Wade wondered why he had been so self-righteous. His own behaviour during the Camino had hardly been a model of virtue.

Marina came over to him. She was smiling.

"Carlos and I are together again. I was puzzled when you told me that there was someone I know downstairs. But thank you!"

"No problem."

"Perhaps we can go shopping later, when Carlos is ready, and buy some food for tonight. It will be our last dinner together before the end of the Camino in Santiago."

Later, after they had been to the supermarket, Maja and Carlos got to work in the kitchen corner at the albergue and produced a fine meal. Seeing them together, working as a team, sharing jokes and touches and glances, Wade had a feeling of satisfaction that in a small way he had contributed to their reconciliation.

In the meantime, Wade and Ayumi laid the table, Philippe produced several bottles of wine and Dante joined them too.

At the adjoining table there was a group of young French pilgrims, who had also just prepared their dinner. A young man was serving soup to the others.

"That smells delicious," Marina said to him.

"Thank you. If you like we can share? We have a lot of soup."

"But you must have some of our food too."

It would be a real party.

Looking around, Wade saw many familiar faces from along the way. Other peregrino families were, like his, preparing to spend this last evening together. They were all talking excitedly, looking forward to the big day ahead.

The only blot on the horizon from Wade's point of view was the corpulent figure of the Alabama Preacher, last seen in Arzúa, standing together with his entourage in the far corner of the vast room and looking a little out of place among the genuine pilgrims – or so Wade thought. But was he being self-righteous again? His own path to Santiago had hardly been very spiritual, but at least he had walked it, every inch of the way, carrying his own bag.

He noticed that Philippe was observing them too.

"I met them in Palas de Rei," Wade said. "I don't like them."

"They have bad vibes," said Philippe simply.

That night, as he lay in his bunk in the darkened dormitory, Wade felt the slight vibration of his mobile phone under his pillow. It was a message from Angelina:

Dear Wade, hope you find some emotional and mental rest in the cathedral tomorrow. Take your time and get some rest, and I think you should go then to finisterre even more now. Didn't you tell me you don't give up once you've started something, no?

Bring me a shell. Bad headache day today, but I'm ok. X

He thought for a few moments before tapping a message back:

You're right. I must walk on to end. But first i will pray for you in the cathedral. Love Wade x

The reply from Angelina came almost immediately:

:) I knew you wouldn't give up. Walk for yourself. x

Wade smiled to himself in the darkness and texted back:

I will :) xxx

*

Many pilgrims at the albergue were already on their way by daybreak. It was only about twenty kilometres to Santiago and they wanted to reach their goal in time for the pilgrims' mass in the cathedral at midday. Dante was one of those who left early, but Wade and the rest of his friends didn't set off until after a leisurely breakfast.

"There is a pilgrims' mass every day at twelve," said Carlos. "We can do it tomorrow. Today we can enjoy the walk together, get our Compostelas, have a late lunch at Casa Manolo and celebrate some more in Santiago this evening. What do you think?"

"Sounds like a good plan," said Wade. "But what exactly is Casa Manolo?"

"I was there when I did the Camino two years ago. It's a restaurant popular with the pilgrims and many go there for a meal to celebrate their arrival in Santiago at last. It can be crowded, but it's not expensive."

So it was the five of them – Carlos, Marina, Philippe, Ayumi and Wade – who set out together on this, the final short stage of the Camino de Santiago. Though the weather was cold, the sun shone down from a pale blue sky as usual.

Wade glanced upwards. "Thank you, God," he whispered to himself.

There were many pilgrims on the way now and after a while, they caught up with the Alabama Preacher and his followers, who greeted them cheerily as they passed by. Wade wondered if he had maybe misjudged them. He was feeling at his most charitable.

Wade and his friends were walking briskly, keen to reach Santiago at last. They were walking on roads now, but there was little traffic – just a few cars, a bus and a couple of taxis went by, but nothing else. It was some time since they had overtaken the Alabama Preacher, so Wade was surprised to see him standing at the roadside some way ahead – that is until he noticed the nearby bus stop. He was alone, so he had presumably taken the bus for a few kilometres and was now waiting for his entourage to catch up. He gave them a cheery wave as they walked by.

"He can't even manage the last few kilometres without cheating," Wade muttered to himself under his breath.

When approaching Santiago, many of the pilgrims hurried on along the road, anxious to reach their goal as quickly as possible.

"We should not do that," said Carlos. "The pilgrim tradition is to walk up to the top of the hill at Monte do Gozo – the mount of joy. There you will see a wonderful view across Santiago to the distant cathedral."

At the top of the hill was a large, pyramid-like monument which had been erected to commemorate the visit of Pope John Paul II some years before. The lower surfaces of the structure were covered in pilgrim graffiti – prayers and many messages. Philippe, who was there with his marker pen, saw Wade watching him."

"I am writing a message for Gabriella," he said. "Maybe she will see it this time, maybe not."

"Have you left messages before then?" Wade asked.

"Yes, some days ago when I was walking alone along a stony path, I had the idea to leave her a message. I spent maybe an hour collecting stones and laying them on the ground to form the name 'Gabriella', but I found out later she didn't see it. Then at the hundred-kilometre waymark, I wrote her another message and she found that one. If she comes this way, she may find this, but in any case, I will be there to meet her in Santiago when she arrives."

Soon they all moved on to the imposing statues of two pilgrims looking out over the city and pointing towards the spires of the cathedral on the skyline. Now that their goal was literally in sight, they were excited at the prospect and eager to reach the cathedral square without further delay.

If anything, Carlos, who had been to Santiago before, was the most excited of them all. He led the way down the hill and onwards to the busy road which would take them to the city itself; but by the time they eventually reached the ancient, pilgrims' way into Santiago – the Rúa de San Pedro – they didn't need a guide, yellow arrows, or waymarks any more. There were other pilgrims within sight in front of them and people they met in the narrow, cobbled street would often smile and point them in the right direction. As they waited to cross the busy street at the Porta do Camino, the traditional entry point for pilgrims to the old city, Wade suddenly thought of a biblical saying that he had learned as a boy in Sunday School: 'Straight is the gate and narrow is the way that leadeth unto righteousness.'

They were entering the last metres now, with a short, stone-paved incline up to the Praza de Cervantes, then bearing right and descending the final slope to the cathedral square.

"Look! There's the cathedral, just on the left," said Marina.

"I know, but we have to go through the archway straight ahead to the main square," said Carlos.

As they reached the tunnel-like passageway, where a street musician was playing bagpipes on the dark steps leading down to the sunlit cathedral square at the other end, Wade suddenly remembered something that Eduardo had once told him about this moment. He was leading the way now, walking out of the tunnel and straight across to the middle of the vast, paved square – the Praza do Obradoiro. Only when he reached its centre, did he turn round to face the cathedral.

The five friends stood together, staring in wonder at the magnificent Baroque facade of the cathedral, whose soaring towers dominated the ancient city. No matter if one of the towers was surrounded in scaffolding, it did little to diminish this awe-inspiring sight. The friends huddled closer, in a communal embrace, heads together, their eyes brimming with tears, whispering over and over, "Thank you! Thank you!" They shared a feeling of intense joy and togetherness, a wondrous moment that none of them would ever forget and which could never be repeated.

Other pilgrims they knew were arriving in the huge cathedral square too. They congratulated each other, they kissed, they hugged, they took photos. Nobody wanted to move on, but eventually, they drifted off to the nearby Pilgrims' Office to collect their Compostelas. There was a short queue of other pilgrims all waiting to do the same.

"In the summer months I believe there are so many pilgrims that they have to stand in line for hours," said Carlos.

Once inside the office, they were each given a form to fill out.

Marina touched Wade on the shoulder. "Don't forget, you must put a tick against religious or spiritual reasons in order to get the Latin Compostela."

Wade turned and smiled. "Thank you, I've already done it."

While they were waiting, Wade noticed a corpulent figure standing next to the counter and talking to Carlos. It was the Alabama Preacher.

"I want the Compostela to be in the name of my

church in Alabama, where I am the Pastor," he declared in an unnecessarily loud voice to the clerk behind the counter.

The clerk patiently explained to him that the Compostela had to be in his own name, which, with apparent reluctance, he eventually accepted.

"What a hypocrite!" Wade muttered to Marina. "He did most of his short Camino by bus or taxi. He's not even entitled to a Compostela. I only hope Carlos doesn't invite him to eat with us at Casa Manolo."

Marina laughed. "I do not think you need to worry about that," she said.

Later on, after their meal at Casa Manolo, the five friends split up for the time being. Carlos and Marina had called ahead the previous evening to book a double room at a pension some distance from the city centre, Philippe would be staying at the albergue in Hospedería San Martín Pinario on the north side of the cathedral until Gabriella finally arrived, while Ayumi went off to find a pension recommended to her by Japanese friends. They all arranged to meet in the centre of the cathedral square that evening at eight.

Wade picked up his backpack and strolled slowly back towards the cathedral. He wanted to find a room as close as possible to this magnificent building and feel its aura around him.

Now, at the end of November, there were relatively few pilgrims or tourists in Santiago and he soon found a pension near the cathedral at a good price. The young lady, Maria, who showed him the room was friendly, with a beautiful smile and she spoke good English.

"Do you know Santiago?" she asked him.

"No, I just finished the Camino today and I've never been here before."

"Then you should take this map of the city. Everything you want is very near. Look, here in the Rua do Franco are many bars and restaurants," she said, marking them on the map with a pen.

"Great. That will be useful later. I'm meeting up with my friends at eight o'clock to celebrate." He paused a moment. "Would you like to join us?"

She smiled. "Thank you, but no. I have a sore throat and a cold and I need to go home to bed."

He smiled back at her. "That's a pity. Oh, one more thing before I forget. I need to use the internet, so can you tell me where I can find an internet café?"

"Of course," she said, marking a cross on the map. "But I can do better than that. In the office, I have a laptop and I rarely use it. You can borrow it while you're here. I will get it for you and give you the code."

As he lay on the bed of his room, after taking a shower and changing his clothes, Wade listened to the sounds of the street outside. There was music coming from the tunnel that led to the square, where the street musicians played and sang. Then the cathedral clock struck seven and he could hear the voice of an angel singing 'Nessun Dorma'. Even the buskers here were extra class, and when she hit the final 'Vincero! Vincero! Vincero!' he began to cry and couldn't stop, just like when he was on the meseta.

Eventually, he calmed down enough to send a text to Angelina:

We made it, and it was a moment of intense emotion. I'm flying high, haven't come down to earth yet. Love Wade

7. SANTIAGO DE

COMPOSTELA

He got up and peered out of the window at the street below. Early pilgrims were walking by in the sunshine, eager to reach the cathedral square and the culmination of a journey they would never forget.

Having spent the previous evening celebrating with his friends in the bars of the old city, Wade hadn't woken up until much later than he usually did on the Camino. Even so, it felt strange not to be donning his backpack ready to start the day's walk. Instead, he had a couple of hours to relax before meeting the others again in front of the cathedral. He picked up his mobile and sent texts to his son and daughter announcing his arrival in Santiago. Then he noticed there was a new message from Angelina:

Many congratulations! Enjoy santiago! Bad headache day, so can't write much. x

He got back into bed where, armed with Maria's laptop, he propped himself up on the pillows and composed an email to Angelina:

Dear Angelina

I'm so sorry that you're still suffering from headaches. The "little" concussion you mentioned is clearly bigger than you thought initially. Take it easy if you can. I will say a prayer for you in the cathedral today. Maybe it will help.

The five of us who arrived here together yesterday are all going to the pilgrims' mass together at noon today. We also spent yesterday evening together and will be together this evening too. For the moment we are joined as if by some invisible umbilical cord, but tomorrow we'll be splitting up and going our different ways.

I'm staying at a pension here in Santiago, just around the corner from the cathedral square, as I've had enough of albergues for a few days at least. But I intend to leave for Finisterre soon before my resolve weakens. Old Santiago is a fantastic city, and yesterday we were in a Tapas bar that reminded me of our last evening together in Burgos. Later, we moved on to another bar and who should we meet up with but Min-Joo and Chu-Young. It was lovely to see them once more before they depart from Spain.

I learned from them that Danilo and Maja are on their way to Finisterre now, but by the time they return to Santiago I'll probably be on the same journey. It takes 3 or 4 days to Finisterre apparently and you have to cope with it being lonelier than the Camino de Frances. Then, when I get back here it will be time to go back home I expect. I must book my plane today.

Wish I could have done it all with you though.

Take care. Get well soon.

With my love

Wade x

PS; Attached is a photo I just got from Chu-Young. It was taken last night in Santiago when we all met up in a bar. The one looking like Father Christmas is me! I don't know how much longer I'll keep the beard.

When he finally dragged himself out of bed, there was just time to go for a coffee prior to meeting up with his friends again. There was a bar just around the corner, and he sat at a table near the window overlooking the Praza da Quintana, a vast, granite-paved square, with a view to the east facade of the imposing cathedral. The bar was empty except for a dark-haired, middle-aged man sitting at an adjacent table. From his clothing, he was clearly a pilgrim too, but a fashion-conscious one and his face looked vaguely familiar. While Wade was trying to work out where he had seen him before, the man spoke.

"Didn't I see you a few weeks ago in Logroño? There was a party in the albergue."

"Ah yes, I remember now…"

"There was a real nice chick there, name of Angelina, but I didn't have any success."

"I remember that too," said Wade, somewhat coldly.

"She a friend of yours?"

"Yes, she is actually."

"Lucky guy. Nice chick. By the way, I'm Dimitri." He held out his hand.

"My name's Wade." They shook hands. "You have a Greek name, but you sound like you're from the USA."

"Yeah, I was born in Athens, but my family emigrated to the USA when I was a small boy."

Dimitri certainly looked Greek, with a proud nose, slightly olive complexion and black hair. He was an older version of the young guys Wade had got to know in Greece decades before, in that summer of love, when he first met his future wife.

"When did you get into Santiago?"

"Yesterday," said Wade. "It was a fantastic moment when we arrived. I'll never forget it."

"You were with Angelina?"

"No, I was with some other friends that I met along the way. Angelina had to fly home after Burgos."

"That's bad luck. Burgos is usually a good pick-up point."

"What do you mean by that?"

"Well, it's a point on the Camino where a lot of new relationships are cemented, consummated you might say, and if you're lucky you have a sexual partner all the way to Santiago."

Wade was getting annoyed. "That's not why I'm on the Camino, but I would have liked the chance to build a relationship with Angelina. She's a very special person to me."

"Okay, okay, don't get sore. It's good to love each

chick a little, but don't expect the relationship of a lifetime on the Camino. It's just not going to happen."

They were quiet for a few moments. Wade felt slightly irritated by Dimitri. He appeared so cock-sure of himself, brimming with self-confidence, but in reality, he was just an ageing gigolo with the beginning of a middle-age spread and a double chin.

"You seem to be travelling alone too," said Wade at last. "What happened to your pick up in Burgos?"

Dimitri shrugged his shoulders. "No luck this time."

"So you've done this Camino before?"

"Sure. Every fall for the past five years I've come over to Spain for this. It's a good time for the younger chicks. In the summer months, there are too many people, and they're too old, and in the winter it's too cold."

"Is that why you do it? Just for sex?"

"Not just for sex, but it certainly plays a role." Dimitri paused, thoughtfully. "The Camino is an addiction, as you'll probably realise when you have to go back home."

Dimitri glanced at his watch. "I'd better pay up and go. I've booked a massage for this morning. It's a great way to relax after all that walking."

"I've never tried it," said Wade.

"Is that so? Well, I can recommend it. Have you got a city map?" Wade gave him his map. "Right, the massage parlour's not in the old city, but if you walk from the big square, 'Praza de Galicia', it's only about ten minutes or so from there. Look, I'll mark the direction on your map with an arrow, and this is the exact address and phone number." He scribbled the information on the edge of the map.

"Hmmm... do they speak English?"

"Not a lot, but enough. If you like I can make an appointment for you while I'm there. Give me your cell phone number and I'll send you a text."

Despite having a few doubts, Wade gave Dimitri his number anyway. It would be a new experience, and if he changed his mind about the massage... well he just wouldn't turn up.

"Okay! When's the best time for you?" said Dimitri as he saved the number. "Morning or afternoon? They're likely to be too busy in the evening."

"It would have to be sometime tomorrow afternoon. I'm leaving for Finisterre the day after."

"Good, I'll fix it. I'll be in touch later. Buen Camino!"

As Wade walked round to the other side of the cathedral, where he was to meet his friends, he wondered briefly why Dimitri was so keen to help him. He arrived at the meeting point just as the bells were chiming the hour. The other four were waiting for him.

"The pilgrims' mass will be crowded," said Carlos. "We should go in now if we want to get good seats."

Wade had hoped to have a proper breakfast before going into the cathedral, but Carlos was right. Pilgrims were already flocking in, but the five friends just managed to find a pew where they could all sit together and have a good view of the famed

Botafumeiro censer when it swung into action. Then, by twelve o'clock the pews were full and many people even had to stand in the side aisles, trying to peer round the massive stone columns that supported the roof structure.

Wade noticed the bulky figure of the Alabama Preacher, sitting towards the front at the end of a pew on the other side of the main aisle. An elderly Spanish lady with a stick was standing nearby and when the Alabama Preacher saw her, he stood up with a smile and gave her his seat. Wade wondered again if he had misjudged the man, and who was he to judge anybody anyway.

He looked around him at the congregation. "They're not all pilgrims, that's for sure."

"No," said Carlos. "Some of them are tourists and the cathedral is a big attraction. There are also many local people of course."

Wade found the service interesting, but not as moving as he had expected. There was a nun with a beautiful voice who led the singing and chanting, but Wade felt a little disappointed that there was no choir.

After the taking of the sacrament, the service came slowly to an end and they waited impatiently to see the famous Botafumeiro censer swing into action. – but it didn't. Nothing happened.

"It seems nobody sponsored it today," said Carlos.

"What do you mean?" Wade replied.

"It takes eight guys to swing the Botafumeiro and someone has to pay for them."

As they left the cathedral and emerged into the

pale sunlight they expressed their disappointment. Philippe, who had been three months walking from Geneva, said jokingly: "Two thousand kilometres – for nothing!" They all laughed.

Like the others, Wade had put his mobile phone on 'silent mode' while they were in the cathedral. Now, when he reset it, he saw that he had received a new message. He checked it and saw it was from his daughter:

Wow! Many congratulations! I'm so proud of you. Love J xxx

Wade felt quite emotional as he read it and bit his lip to fight back the tears. His children were adults now, but they remained his great joy. Though he had achieved little in material terms, and in his darker moments, he might look back at the thirty years spent in Frankfurt as a life wasted, in his heart he knew that it was his children that had made his time there worthwhile.

Over the years he and Sabina had grown apart until eventually, she had found someone who was prepared to put her first. The marriage was finally over, but the children were still quite young then and Wade had stayed on in Frankfurt to be near them, living alone in a small apartment near to what had been, for so many years, the family home. In a way, it was too near, literally just around the corner, but he had suffered in silence and it had enabled him to keep in close contact with his children. At the same time, he had closed his heart to any idea of looking for another woman. It only brought suffering. Enough was enough.

After his retirement, when the children had left home, he had returned to London see out his days in the place where he belonged. But did he really belong anywhere after thirty years in exile?

He was interrupted in his thoughts by the buzz of his mobile as another message came through:

I booked your massage for 2:00 pm tomorrow. Enjoy! Dimitri

Later in the day, the five friends met up once more for a final evening of red wine and tapas in the Taberna do Bispo. The family was breaking up, and they were uncertain about whether or not they would all meet again. Carlos and Marina would begin walking to Finisterre the next morning, Ayumi would spend one more day in Santiago before flying back home, while Philippe had decided to continue waiting for Gabriella in Santiago and then walk with her to Finisterre later.

"What about you, Wade?" Marina asked. "Will you walk on to Finisterre too?"

"Yes, but not tomorrow. Er...I want to rest up a little longer and spend some more time in the cathedral."

"And after Finisterre?"

"I may have time for a couple of nights in Santiago before going back home, depending on how long it takes me to do the walk. I booked my flight to London this afternoon, so I've got a deadline now."

At the end of the evening, they all went back to the very centre of the cathedral square and clung together in a communal hug with whispers of, "Take care! Buen Camino!"

*

During the night Wade needed to go to the toilet. It was a luxury to have his own bathroom en-suite at the pension, instead of having to find his way along cold, dark corridors in some draughty albergue. As he got out of bed and climbed to his feet he suddenly felt the room spinning round and had to sit down on the edge of the bed until it stopped. He was also feeling slightly nauseous.

"Too much to drink," he muttered to himself as he eventually shuffled off to the bathroom.

He was glad to be spending another day in Santiago. He obviously needed the break physically, but he also wanted to visit the cathedral once more and spend some quiet moments there.

After a late breakfast at the bar just round the corner from his pension, where he had met Dimitri the day before, Wade strolled on to the north entrance of the cathedral and went in. There were few visitors about so he was able to better appreciate the splendour of the building. He visited the crypt and saw the ornate chest containing the relics of St James; then he climbed the steps to a small chamber behind the high altar, in order to embrace the effigy of the saint (an old pilgrim tradition). Finally, he entered a small chapel he had caught a glimpse of the previous day – Capilla del Santísimo.

The approach to the small chapel was marked by a lobby and a large glass partition which allowed Wade to look inside the chapel before entering it. He could see there was only one person in there. An elderly woman with a veil over her head was kneeling in a front pew, on the right-hand side, with her rosary beads in her hand. Wade entered quietly and knelt in the second row, but on the left-hand side, so that he had an unobstructed view of the altar. He glanced about him at first, allowing himself time to take in his surroundings, and then, once he felt perfectly calm, he closed his eyes:

"God, my God, whoever you are, whatever you are, give me strength to cope with the final part of my pilgrimage and help me to find the spiritual path that I'm seeking. Bless my family and friends and keep them safe. Bless Angelina and help her to get well again. Amen."

When Wade opened his eyes, he found himself gazing at the low, white, marble screen in front of the altar. At the very centre of the latticed screen was a circular section with a diagonal cross, on either side of which he could read the letters A and W. His heart almost stopped. Did the letters signify Angelina and Wade? If so, was it a good sign? Or did the diagonal cross between the letters signify that this love was not to be? Whatever else it might mean, it was clearly a distraction from his efforts to find his spiritual path.

He left the cathedral and walked round to the large sunlit square on the east side – the Praza da Quintana. There were a few people sitting on the granite steps above the square, enjoying the wintry sunshine and Wade, in reflective mood, decided to sit there too. It wasn't long before he sensed a familiar presence at his side.

"So you finally made it to this amazing city with its

splendid cathedral," said Diego. "It's an achievement of sorts."

"What do you mean by that?"

"Well, it's a long walk for an old man and you did it carrying your own bag and walked every step of the way. Respect! It's a physical achievement."

"Nothing else?"

"You tell me! Have you found your spiritual self? Have you at least searched for it diligently? Or have you succumbed to temptation?"

"Stop talking like the bible!" said Wade irritably. "Okay, I've let myself be sidetracked a bit, but this Camino has made me feel like a young man again. It's only natural that I should be interested in women – young women."

Diego chuckled. "You're deluding yourself. Young women are interested in young men and not in old-age pensioners. Surely even you can see that now. What success have you had?"

"Not much, I suppose. But Angelina likes me."

"Yes, as a friend, but I think not as a lover."

"She kissed me like a lover."

Diego sighed. "You'll just have to learn the hard way."

Wade said nothing, but stared fixedly ahead, ignoring the old man. He soon felt cold, in spite of the sunshine, and stood up to leave. Diego had already vanished.

Wade looked at his watch. His massage appointment was still some hours away, so he decided to go back to the pension. Would he keep the appointment later? He didn't know.

Back in his room, he remembered that he hadn't replied yet to Danilo's last email that he had received some days before in Arzúa. This could be his last chance to write before returning Maria's computer. He sat on the bed, leaning back against the headboard and quickly found Danilo's message. He began his reply:

Hi Danilo

I don't get to use a computer very often on this Camino, so I think it's quite a while since I wrote to you.

Congratulations to you and Maja on getting to Santiago. It was a very emotional moment, wasn't it? We arrived a couple of days ago and clung to each other in a circle, everybody crying and saying "Thank you, thank you". I was with Carlos, Philippe, Marina from Italy and Ayumi (Japanese lady).

The mysterious Gabriella hasn't got here yet. Philippe seems very much in love, and he's going to wait for her in Santiago, but he doesn't know exactly where she is and none of us has seen Gabriella for some time. I think she likes to have men chasing after her.

I still have almost daily contact with Angelina. She is a lovely young woman in every way and I wish I were 35 years younger :).

Tomorrow I'm starting for Finisterre and may return to Santiago for a brief visit before my flight to London. I think I'll be ready to go back. Everyone I know from the Camino will have left Santiago by then.

It was great getting to know you and I hope we will keep in touch. A big hug for Maja too. I'm a romantic, so I hope that your Camino together will not be the end, but the start of a long relationship. Invite me to the wedding please!

All the best

Wade

Even though Dimitri had indicated the way to the massage parlour on Wade's city map, it took him some time to find the right street. It wasn't in an area much frequented by tourists, being quite some way from the old city and devoid of any buildings of cultural or historic interest. The street itself was uninviting, particularly as the cold winter rain was now hammering down. Some of the properties appeared to be empty, at least on the ground floor, and the only real signs of life came from the lights of a dubious looking bar in the middle of the block.

Wade was just about to give up when he noticed the illuminated sign, 'Asia Massage', flickering in a window on the first floor, just a little further along the block. There was a large, somewhat tatty-looking entrance door at street level, with an array of bell pushes for the occupants of the floors above. He found the bell push for 'Asia Massage' and pressed it.

"Yes, who is it? Quién es?" came a woman's voice after a few seconds.

Wade stammered something about a massage appointment.

"Come in," said the voice on the intercom and the door opener buzzed.

The door to the massage parlour itself opened off the first-floor landing, where a short but sturdy looking Asian woman in her late forties was waiting to greet him. She was quite heavily made up, with shining red lipstick.

"You come for massage?"

"Yes. Er… my friend Dimitri made an appointment for me."

"Ah! I know. With oil." She smiled and beckoned him inside.

They were now in a large lobby, parts of which were sectioned off into cubicles by heavy curtains reaching from ceiling to floor. At the rear of the lobby was a long couch, on which a woman, in her mid-thirties and clad in shorts and a t-shirt, was reclining provocatively, or so Wade thought. In front of the couch and similarly dressed, another woman was standing hands on hips and presenting her profile to Wade, except for her face which was turned towards him in a big smile.

The woman who had met him at the door was clearly the boss.

"Which one you want?" she asked Wade, gesturing towards the two younger women.

Wade felt embarrassed. This was not what he had expected.

"I… I don't know," he said, feeling his face turn red.

She laughed. "Okay! You go in there please," she said, pulling back the curtain to one of the cubicles.

Wade entered the cubicle and she followed him in. "Take clothes off please and hang them here!" She indicated the clothes stand in the corner and then left him.

Wade looked around. The cubicle was lit by lamps in the ceiling and there were no windows. The walls were plain white and hung with posters showing scenes from Thailand. On the end wall there was a shelf with a Buddha statue and two small vases for incense sticks, while on the right near the entrance, fresh towels and oils had been placed on a further shelf. Dominating the cubicle, placed adjacent to the wall on the left, was a large massage table covered in a white sheet and with small pillows at the far end.

He felt awkward. The hackneyed phrase occurred to him about being 'out of one's comfort zone'. That really summed it up nicely. He got undressed – taking everything off except for his boxer shorts. He had seen videos of massage on YouTube, and they always kept their underpants on.

After a couple of minutes, the woman came in again, carrying a bowl of steaming liquid and warm towels. Now she was dressed just in shorts and a T-shirt too, like her younger colleagues, and she seemed to have applied an extra layer of makeup and lipstick. He was going to be massaged by the boss herself.

She looked at Wade, waiting there in his blue boxer shorts. "Everything off – shorts too please, and lie on the table!"

This was clearly not the same as YouTube – but he did as he was told, took off his shorts and lay face down on the massage table, head on the small pillow. He closed his eyes and waited.

The scent of the incense sticks, which the masseuse had just lit, wafted through the cubicle. Then, Wade felt warm, moist towels being applied to his back, buttocks and legs before the actual massage began. The masseuse hopped up on the massage bank and set to work, pressing, squeezing, pummelling his tired and aching muscles. It was a pleasant experience, and he was feeling quite relaxed until she told him to turn over.

Wade lay on his back now, with eyes open, looking up at the ceiling, but not feeling relaxed anymore. The masseuse seemed to spend an inordinately long time massaging his upper thighs, and occasionally she would accidentally brush against his penis. Or did she do it deliberately? He tried to think of something else.

Suddenly, her face loomed above his. "You want I massage this?" she whispered, holding his hardening penis.

Wade sighed. This was not the sexual experience he had been hoping for during the past few weeks, but it would do. "Okay," he said and closed his eyes again.

Later, as Wade was strolling back through the city, he came across a florist's shop. On the spur of the moment, he went in and bought a single red rose. And when he returned to the pension he presented the rose to Maria.

"It's for your kindness in lending me your laptop," he told her.

"Oh Wade, thank you so much. I will put your lovely rose in a vase right away and keep it here on the desk."

She came round to his side of the desk and kissed him lightly on both cheeks.

"Buen Camino, Wade. I'm sure you will enjoy Finisterre."

"Won't you be here in the morning?"

"No, tomorrow is my day off, but you can leave the key and the laptop with my colleague when you go."

Wade wondered why he had bought the flower. How could his visit to the massage parlour have inspired such a romantic gesture? He just didn't know any more.

As he went upstairs to his room, he heard his mobile phone buzzing in his pocket. He took out the phone to read the incoming message. It was from Dimitri – just two words:

Happy ending?

Wade had arranged to meet Ayumi and Philippe once again that evening for more tapas and red wine at the Taberna do Bispo.

"Philippe, have you heard from Gabriella?" Ayumi asked.

"Yes, she will arrive in Santiago tomorrow and we will walk together to Finisterre in a few days' time."

Philippe was smiling happily and Wade felt a pang of jealousy. But why? Admittedly, he was a bit sad. He would have liked to see Gabriella again, if only to say goodbye, but maybe it was better this way.

"I got a message from Marina tonight," said Ayumi. "She says that nobody is doing the Camino to Finisterre now. She and Carlos walked all day without seeing another pilgrim. It's a different experience."

Wade nervously wondered how he would cope with the silence and the solitude.

When he got back to his room late that evening he sent a text to Angelina:

How are the headaches? Feeling any better? I'm setting off for finisterre in the morning. Marina and carlos set off today. they say no other peregrinos :(. Could be hard. Love wade x

The reply came just a few minutes later:

Do you walk alone? Wow! It's like the first day of the camino. Headache is bad, so couldn't go to mallorca with my friends. :(. Must rest more. I saw some pictures. Finisterre looks wonderful, enjoy! x

He texted straight back:

Sorry about continuing headaches. Must be miserable for you. As for the finisterre camino, it will be lonely i expect. I'm not looking forward to it, but i feel committed somehow. Take it easy, but send me messages when you can. Love wade x

8. TO THE END

The next morning Wade looked out of the window and saw that the sky was clear. He got ready quickly, donned his backpack and was on the way well before eight. The air was chilly, but that was to be expected in early December.

There were only a few people about as he walked down the stone paved street, passing the north side of the cathedral on his left. It was then that he saw her, emerging from the cathedral and coming in his direction. It was Gabriella. She stopped when she saw him and he went up to her. He took off his backpack and they embraced briefly.

"I didn't think you would be here yet," said Wade. "Philippe told us you wouldn't arrive for a day or so."

She gave him a big smile. "I am a magician," she said. "Sometimes I'm here and sometimes I disappear. Actually, I arrived last night. I want to stay here for some days to give my feet a chance to recover, then maybe I will walk to Finisterre."

"With Philippe."

She nodded. "He would like to go as soon as possible, but if I feel I can't walk all that way, I'll go on the bus." She looked at his backpack. "And you are walking to Finisterre now?"

"Yes, I am." He paused, then added: "I didn't think I'd see you again."

She kissed him lightly on the cheek. "I wish you well in all your endeavours, Wade. Buen Camino!"

"Gabriella, I wish you well too and I hope you find what you're looking for."

"Thank you!" she said with a smile before turning away towards the Hospedería San Martín Pinario opposite the cathedral.

Wade guessed that Philippe would be waiting there for her. He stood and watched her all the way to the Hostal door, where she turned around and waved briefly before entering the building.

He remained where he was for a few moments before donning his backpack again and continuing on his way through the tunnel, across the cathedral square, past the impressive Parador Hostal dos Reis Catolicos on the right, then down the narrow Rúa dos Hortas and onwards. He hadn't eaten breakfast yet, so when he came to a bar on the outskirts of the city he stopped briefly for a coffee and a croissant.

Later, as he climbed up and away from Santiago, he looked back towards the distant cathedral. The intervening countryside was a frosty white and a thin mist was hanging over the valley, but directly above him, the sky was blue and full of promise.

"Thank you for that, God," he whispered to himself.

It was a very different Camino to the one he had grown used to on the way to Santiago. Though the route through the pleasant countryside was waymarked, the yellow arrows were fewer and less conspicuous here and he missed his way occasionally. He saw just three other pilgrims the whole day, otherwise, he was quite alone and content not to be part of a group for a change.

He walked for a few hours before at last finding a village with a bar where he could take a lunch break. He sat at a table outside, enjoying a beer in the sunshine, while he checked his mobile for messages, hoping to find one from Angelina – but there was nothing.

Later on, as he approached Negreira where he intended to spend the night, he saw a billboard at the side of the road advertising a hotel, with special room prices for pilgrims and a pilgrims' menu too. He knew that the albergue in Negreira would be open, but here was a chance for a more comfortable night with a decent meal and only just a few hundred metres away. He didn't think the chances of meeting many new people were very great on this trip and the idea of staying in a cold, empty albergue was... well, he had done all that before and didn't like it. There were a few cars parked in front of the Hotel Tamara which stood back from the road on his right-hand side. This place was obviously more for tourists than pilgrims, but he didn't care. He turned to his right, walked straight into the reception and booked a room for the night.

The hotel had every facility he desired except for

the internet, so after he had showered and changed his clothes he sent a text to Angelina before going down to the restaurant for his evening meal:

Checked in at hotel in negreira. it was an easy stage, but i went wrong way 3 times, I'm not safe alone (:. Long stage to olveiroa tomorrow, about 33km. How are you feeling today? Love wade x

Her reply came through while he was still in the hotel restaurant:

Don't fear the challenge, embrace it and walk! You're not alone. God walks with you now, no? And me too. Headaches are better today, finally. But I have to take care, don't want them to come back. Aren't there albergues on way to finisterre? Have you met some new people? Take care x

*

With his spirit cheered by Angelina's message, he set off after an early breakfast at the hotel. He took the main road into Negreira and then followed the marked way along narrow lanes ascending from the town. For the next hour he saw nobody at all, but then ahead of him, sitting on a grassy bank in the sunshine at the edge of a small grove of trees, he noticed a young, dark-haired man smoking a pipe. He reminded Wade of a hobbit, but without the hairy feet, and as he drew nearer, the young man's face seemed vaguely familiar.

"Hola!" said the young man as Wade approached. "We know us, yes?"

"Hola! Yes, of course. You are Marcos, I met you one time with Texas Luke. So you are walking to Finisterre too?"

"Sí, to Fisterra. That is the name in Galician. How you like this Camino? Is different to the first one, yes?"

"Sure, it's just as beautiful but much quieter. You're almost the first peregrino I've met since leaving Santiago."

"Is because now is December. Nobody walk to Fisterra in December. Last night at the albergue in Negreira I was the only peregrino. But is no problem for me to be alone. God is always with me. You believe in God, amigo?"

"I'm not sure," said Wade. "I feel that God is real, but I have some problems with the details of Christianity."

"Keep it simple, amigo! For me, God is God – spirit of the universe – and God is good. Is not possible to explain. Just believe and live a good life is enough."

"But enough for what?" said Wade. "Do you believe in an afterlife?"

Marcos shrugged his shoulders. "The universe is everything – that is all we know for sure. Is enough for me."

They walked together as far as Santa Marina and enjoyed a late lunch at a bar before finally parting company. His young companion was in conversation with two local men and didn't seem in any hurry to leave, but Wade wanted to press on and reach Olveiroa before it grew dark and there were at least twelve kilometres to go. He donned his backpack, ready to leave.

"Buen Camino!" said Marcos as they shook hands. "We see us tonight maybe at albergue in Olveiroa?"

"Yes, of course. Buen Camino!"

As Wade reached the door, Marcos called out to him: "Remember, amigo! Keep it simple and just believe!"

Wade walked briskly on, making steady progress and thinking about what Marcos had said. He remembered a passage from the Bible that he had learned as a child.

"God is a spirit and they that worship him must worship him in spirit and in truth," he murmured to himself. "God is the spirit of the universe."

For much of the time, the route followed a narrow country lane, but there was very little traffic. Suddenly, he came upon a yellow arrow which directed him away from the lane towards a broad, rutted farm track which branched off to the left, straight up a steep hill. He stopped for a moment and considered whether or not to simply follow the lane for the remaining few kilometres until he reached Olveiroa, but then he decided to follow the farm track. After all, it might be a shorter way and would certainly be completely traffic free.

It was hard work climbing up the hill on the rutted track, but at least it kept him warm. It was late afternoon now, the sun was sinking fast and the air was growing colder. He was looking forward to a hot shower, a cold beer and a good rest at the albergue.

The way up seemed never ending, but eventually, he reached the top of the hill where he found a damaged, concrete waymark lying on its side at the edge of the track, as if it had been knocked over at some time in the past by a tractor. He looked at the waymark doubtfully. The sun was rapidly disappearing in the west, and that was more or less the direction he wanted. He was faced with a choice of two paths – one to the left going due east, and the other to the right along the ridge of the hill. He turned right, walking briskly, looking in vain for further waymarks to reassure him.

The path continued towards a line of huge wind turbines, with their rotors whirling rapidly in the cold wind that was blowing up on the hill crest. There seemed no end to them and he gradually realised that the path was slowly changing its direction, away from the sunset and more to the south-west.

Something had gone badly wrong. Maybe this had once been a Camino route, but it clearly wasn't anymore. The sun had almost gone now. It would soon be dark, and here he was, tired and quite lost, stuck on top of an isolated, Galician mountain in the middle of a wind farm installation. He was standing near the concrete column supporting one of the huge wind turbines, whose rotor blades humming overhead seemed to be mocking him.

Wade was suddenly filled with an anger he had rarely known – the anger of despair. "Shut up, you fucking windmill! Fuck you! Fuck you!" he screamed at the top of his voice and kicked the concrete column viciously. It was quite painful, but it brought him back to his senses and his anger subsided.

Then he laughed. "I'm tilting at windmills," he shouted, and he began to sing. "My name's Don Quixote, the man from La Mancha."

Having finally regained his composure, he could just see what looked like a small farm far away to the right at the bottom of the hill, and he decided to head towards it, path or no path. He stumbled his way downhill in the semi-darkness, slipping and sliding and hampered by his heavy backpack. But at last, he reached the narrow lane approaching the farm buildings and heard the sound of barking dogs. As he drew nearer, he saw an old man standing in the doorway of the farmhouse and looking in his direction.

Wade went up to him. "Hola! Do you speak English?"

The old man looked at him blankly and shrugged his shoulders. Wade realised he would have to try and communicate with hands and feet and the few words of Spanish that he had picked up during his pilgrimage.

"Me lost – perdido!" he said, gesticulating wildly. "Where is the Camino? Dónde está el Camino de Fisterra?" He pointed in various directions in turn. "Está aquí? O aquí? Dónde está?"

The old man replied in rapid Spanish and pointed along the lane. Wade picked up the words 'todo recto', but what did that mean? He wasn't sure, but from the old man's gestures, he thought it must be straight on.

"How far? One kilometre, two, three, or more?" Wade asked him, signalling the distances with his fingers.

The old man nodded that he understood and held up five fingers. "Cinco kilometros."

"Cinco? That's five isn't it?" said Wade, holding up five fingers.

"Sí, sí. Cinco kilometros."

Wade turned to go. "Gracias," he said.

"Buen Camino!"

Wade walked on, but he felt in need of some reassurance that he was really on the right way now and after about twenty minutes he came to another isolated farmhouse. Dogs were barking here too, though he couldn't see them. A woman was standing at an upstairs window looking down at him. He waved to catch her attention, before going to the front door and knocking loudly. When the woman eventually came to the door, he went through his pantomime act again to confirm his direction. He was on the right way.

He trudged on and on. The shadowy landscape was revealed only by the pale light of the moon. He could just see enough to follow the narrow lane and he felt quite exhausted and alone in the world. Suddenly, ahead of him, he saw a light. He was coming to a junction, where his lane fed into a proper asphalted road with buildings and some traffic, and there at the junction he saw a sign indicating Olveiroa to the right, but it was still five kilometres away. He never seemed to get any nearer no matter how far he walked. Just to the left, on the opposite side of the road, was a workshop of some sort where a man was locking up for the night. Further along the road, he could see the lights of a village.

Wade crossed the road to speak to the man. "Aquí Albergue? Pension? Hotel?" he asked with some desperation in his voice as he pointed towards the village.

"Sí!" the man answered. "Hay un hotel."

He indicated the right-hand side of the road where an illuminated sign was just visible in the distance.

"Gracias! Gracias!" said Wade and set off with renewed energy towards the beckoning lights.

*

He awoke the next morning at the hotel, in a warm room, in a comfortable bed, feeling more or less recovered from his exertions of the previous day when he had strayed far from the way. He was some kilometres short of Olveiroa, but at least he knew how to get there now. He had been too exhausted the previous evening to send Angelina a message, so before getting up Wade reached for his mobile on the bedside table and texted a short update to her.

He was ready to leave the hotel about seven, after a good breakfast, and he went into the bar to pay his bill. The pretty girl working there could speak a little English and offered to drive him into Olveiroa later. Wade was tempted, but he was determined, even now, to walk every inch of the way to Finisterre.

"Muchas gracias! But I must walk. I'm on the Camino."

"It's okay. Take you to Olveiroa in the car. Free. No must pay."

Wade smiled. "It's very kind of you, but I have to walk. No bus, no car, no taxi – only on foot. It's my Camino." He hoped she had understood him. He couldn't remember ever turning down a lift from a pretty girl before.

It was less than an hour's walk along the side of

the busy road to Olveiroa. At least, it seemed to Wade like it was a busy road after the relative isolation of his route for the past couple of days. He was feeling a little apprehensive about the way ahead after his experiences the previous day, though he was determined to go on to the end. He was tired, he had arthritic pains in his left hip, and the big toe of his right foot had been hurting ever since he had kicked the wind turbine. He just wanted to finally get to Finisterre and then stop. Suddenly he felt his mobile phone vibrating in his pocket and hoped it would be a message from Angelina. It was:

Wow, this is the real adventure! Not for arrow pilgrims. You must have walked 40 to 50 km yesterday. Hope you don't feel too lonely, but indeed it can be nice to be alone after all the group things. Cross my fingers that you find the right way today. x

Wade smiled to himself and gently kissed the screen of the phone. That simple message had perked him up and he walked on with renewed vigour.

He stopped briefly in Olveiroa to get a bottle of mineral water and a bocadillo for the day's trek and then continued, climbing gradually upwards until he reached the parting of the ways just beyond the village of Hospital. It was a road junction, with the way to Finisterre signed to the left and the road to Muxia to the right. He took the way to the left and followed the road for a few minutes until he came at last to a waymark indicating a track to his right, which would take him across the high plain and eventually down to the coast at Cee.

He was soon walking through a splendid open landscape, with not a soul or building in sight. Wind turbines on the surrounding hills were today turning gently and silently. The winds of the previous day had died down and the sunshine felt warm enough for Wade to remove his jacket and pullover.

Approaching the highest point of this stage, he saw a waymark at the edge of the stony track. As he neared the waymark, he could see that someone had covered the side that faced him with green paint together with the words 'TO THE END' painted in yellow capital letters. Nearer still, he noticed that the adjacent side was painted orange, with the words 'TO THE TRUTH' painted in black and a spiral symbol with an arrow pointing along the track ahead. What did it all mean? Finisterre would certainly be the end of his Camino, but would he find the truth there?

Wade stopped here to rest for a few minutes before beginning the descent towards Cee and it wasn't long before he caught his first glimpse of the ocean, looming out of the mist on the horizon. The stony track descended steeply and seemingly without end. Wade, who was beginning to feel strangely weak, was making slow progress. His feet hurt, his knees hurt, his left hip hurt. This was nothing new, but normally he was able to relegate these aches and pains to the back of his mind where he hardly noticed them. He was sweating, but it was a cold sweat, and he had a headache. It was almost like sunstroke but in December? He thought he might faint at any moment. What was wrong with him? He felt quite disoriented.

Somehow Wade made it down to Cee. He had originally intended to walk on to Corcubión, but now all he wanted was to find somewhere quiet and comfortable to rest and recover. As he struggled through the narrow streets of the sleepy town he soon found a small hotel with a room available. He checked in and went up to his room, where he forced himself to get undressed and take a shower before crawling exhausted into bed.

*

Wade was didn't feel any better the next morning, after a bad night with his aching limbs keeping him awake, so he decided to rest up a bit longer and stay another night in Cee.

After a light breakfast in the hotel restaurant, he returned to his room where he spent most of the morning just lying on his bed. Eventually, about midday, he felt well enough to venture outside for a gentle stroll in the town. It was cold outside and before long he entered a bar to keep warm and drink a coffee. He sat down at a table by the window, facing the promenade, where he could see the people walking by outside. He had always enjoyed people-watching and it required little effort on his part.

Wade was on his second cup of coffee when he saw her – a young woman with a shapely figure, strolling along the promenade with an older man. They were almost opposite the bar before Wade realised that he knew the young woman with her long, dark hair and piercing blue eyes. It was Maja, but she wasn't with Danilo. The man with her was old enough to be her father. Wade knocked hard on the window to draw her attention, and when she saw him she smiled, waved and exchanged a few words with her companion before coming into the bar alone. Wade stood up to greet her and Maja gave him a big hug.

"Wade, this is a great surprise. It's good to see you again. My friend, Pedro, has brought me here in his car today. I'm staying in Finisterre actually. I love to be by the sea."

"I'm on my way to Finisterre," said Wade. "I want to walk there tomorrow."

"You must stay at the Albergue Cabo da Vila. The people are very nice there."

"Okay, I'll do that. Er… what's happened to Danilo?" he asked cautiously.

Maja smiled, but a little sadly this time. "I'm afraid we split up again. Danilo wanted to go to Andalusia and walk some more, but once I got to Finisterre I just wanted to stay."

"I'm very sorry you've split with Danilo," said Wade. "And Pedro?"

"He's a friend, that's all. He's lives in Finisterre but he has some business here in Cee, so he offered to bring me here this morning."

"I see. Do you have you time for a coffee?" Wade asked, noticing that the waiter was hovering nearby.

"Not really." Maja nodded towards Pedro, who was waiting outside in the street. "But if you come to the Albergue Cabo da Vila tomorrow, I may see you there. I am staying there another day before going on to Muxia."

With a smile and an embrace she left and went to join Pedro outside. She turned briefly to wave to Wade before she and her friend strolled on along the promenade.

That evening Wade felt well enough to eat a

decent dinner at his hotel. His aches and pains had subsided and he was ready to complete the Camino the next day. He went to bed quite early, but before switching off the light he sent Angelina a text:

Hi Angelina, not reached the end of the earth yet. I wasn't feeling too well, so i spent a day resting here in cee, but i'm ok now and will walk the final stage tomorrow. I wish we were doing it together :). Will write again when i get to finisterre. Hope you are still headache free. Love Wade x.

*

The fine winter weather that had accompanied Wade for much of his Camino stayed true to the end. He set off early, walking at a leisurely pace, enjoying the view over a tranquil sea which glistened in the sunlight. His right foot was pretty sore, but it was his own fault for kicking that wind turbine. Otherwise, he felt quite well again.

The way wasn't too severe, although after Corcubión it climbed up from the sea along stony paths and through wooded areas, crossing the headland before descending again to the coast.

On the way up to the headland, Wade stopped to get his breath back and to admire the view. As he turned to continue his climb he saw a lone magpie hopping about at the edge of the track some way ahead. He remembered the old saying, 'one for sorrow, two for joy', but he looked in vain for a second magpie.

"Just another superstition," he mumbled to himself – but was it?

He recalled something his father had said decades before. It was after his father had been diagnosed with cancer, and was recuperating from an operation which had involved the removal of his left eye. He and Wade had been taking a gentle stroll on Hampstead Heath, in the quiet of an early spring morning, when his father had suddenly stopped and pointed ahead, staring hard at a bird he could see hopping around in the grassy meadow in front of them.

"Look, Wade! It's a magpie. Can you see another?"

"No, Dad, there's only the one."

"A lone magpie is a sign of death," his father had replied quietly.

Within a few weeks, the cancer had returned and his father had died shortly afterwards. He was only sixty years old.

As Wade was nearing Finisterre, he walked past the golden, sandy beach and approached the old town. The main road forked to the right, towards the lighthouse, but ahead of him in the narrow street leading to the old town he saw the sign of the Albergue Cabo da Vila, where he was greeted with a big smile by the hospitalera at the door.

"Hola! You are looking for somewhere to stay? Come in, please."

They entered the reception area which was roomy and bright. Wade noticed some computers set up for guests to use on one side.

"It is very quiet here at the moment. There are not many peregrinos in December. You can have a bed in the albergue on the ground floor, or we can give you an individual room upstairs at a good price, and breakfast is included."

"That sounds fine," Wade replied. "But first can you tell me if a young woman from Austria is staying here? Her name is Maja."

The hospitalera laughed. "It is a beautiful name, but tell me, is she a beautiful woman?"

Wade felt himself blushing. "Yes, she is, very."

"Si, that is our bonita. She left this morning to go to Muxia, but she will come back again, maybe tomorrow."

Wade was disappointed to miss Maja, but pleased with his room situated at the end of a short corridor on the second floor. It had a double bed, a window overlooking the street and was next to the bathroom which he had to himself. He was tired after his morning walk, so after showering, he lay on the bed for a short rest and soon fell asleep.

When Wade woke up it was already mid-afternoon and he wanted to pick up his 'Finisterrana' certificate before walking as far as the lighthouse to see the sunset and complete his journey. The office was located nearby and it only took him a few minutes to collect the certificate and return to the Albergue Cabo da Vila, where he helped himself to a coffee from the machine in reception before setting off.

The way was longer than he had anticipated, or was it just that he felt so incredibly weary? He trudged on until at last the lighthouse came into view. There were just a few other people there, standing on the rocks, looking out over the shimmering sea and waiting for the sunset. It was a glorious sight and he stood watching silently, while the sun turned red as it neared the horizon.

He walked back into town, where he stopped at a bar shortly before reaching the albergue. He ordered a beer and remembered he hadn't yet told Angelina that he had arrived. He sent her a text:

Finisterre at last and it's beautiful. you should visit this place. Will return to santiago by bus. no more walking! my feet are grateful. will write more later. Very tired now camino is over. Lots of love. Wade x

After a few minutes he received Angelina's reply:

I will one day. Congratulations! Drink an extra glass of wine tonight! Was it worth all that walking in the end? Just a few days left before your flight. What are your plans? x

Yes, what were his plans? He pondered this question as he finished his beer. He had learned some hard lessons on the way to Santiago and he had lost track of his spiritual goal, at least until near the end of his Camino. He needed to find his God, and this had to be his plan for the future. But in spite of Diego's warning voice, he still loved this young woman though he hardly knew her. He had to tell her.

Back at the albergue, the hospitalera was in reception when he arrived. Wade greeted her and asked if he could use one of the computers.

"Yes, of course, it's no problem," she answered. "You are the only peregrino here at the moment."

"Really!" said Wade and added: "Have you heard from Maja?"

The hospitalera smiled. "No, nothing yet, but I think she comes back tomorrow.."

Wade went online and started to compose an email to Angelina:

Hi Angelina

You asked about my plans now. It's a difficult question to answer.

I've got mixed feelings about returning home. My daughter will be going to spend Christmas in Germany at her mother's place, while my son will be celebrating with his in-laws as usual. So Christmas day I'll be on my own I expect, though I've been invited by friends in London to go there for New Year. Maybe I can get a place on a Retreat again and meditate for a few days like I did a couple of Christmases ago.

And then what? Time is growing short and whatever I want to do, I must do it now while I'm still active instead of putting it off until some vague future date.

That much at least I have learned from the Camino. I've learned to be more open in my relationships too, though I feel I may have missed the point of your advice to open up my heart. Instead, I've been chasing after women who are too young for me, and that can only lead to suffering I think. I remember telling you about the time when I was in Greece, all those years ago, when I spent the summer on the beaches, looking for girls. It was fun and I had some success — in fact, I got to know my future wife there — but of course, the same tactics don't work any more

The trouble is, the more I think about it, the more I realise that I had already given my heart to you. It was your tender kisses that night in Burgos that reminded me of what I had long forgotten. and I fell in love with you.

I remember I cried for much of the next two days, walking alone, on the Meseta. I couldn't explain why, but I believe now that it was because I realised the hopelessness of the situation. I regretted all those wasted years since my marriage broke up, I regretted not having met an Angelina when I was younger.

With love

Wade x

PS I will bring back a shell for you from Fisterra. You can buy perfect shells in the shops here, but I think it will mean more if I find my own shell on the beach. But when can I give it to you? I don't know.

*

After a late breakfast the next morning he strolled to the beach and took off his sandals. Then he walked to the shoreline, where the sea lapped gently on the sand, and rolled up his trousers to avoid getting the bottoms wet. The hospitalera had done his laundry for him the day before, so now he had all clean clothes and he wanted to keep them that way just a little longer.

As he looked down, searching for a suitable shell to give to Angelina, and listening to the rippling waters, he was reminded of a verse in a poem he had first read in his schooldays. It was something about growing old, strolling on the beach, and hearing the mermaids singing – but not to him. He had never really appreciated the significance of it until now.

"Prufrock," he muttered to himself. "That's who I am – Prufrock."

It wasn't difficult to find a suitable shell – in fact he found quite a number. But he only wanted one, so he laid them out on the sand in the form of a heart and put the one he liked best at its centre. This was the shell he would give to Angelina – if he ever saw her again.

Back in the town, he went to the tourist office,

which was near the bus stop, to check on bus times to Santiago the following day. He had originally intended to spend his last night back in Santiago, before catching his plane in the evening, but now it was too much effort somehow. The clerk in the office gave him a timetable, which Wade looked at briefly.

"I need to be at Santiago airport by six o'clock tomorrow evening," he said. "Do I have to get the first bus, or will the one at midday be early enough?"

"There is a good service from Santiago bus station to the airport. Every thirty minutes. You don't need to leave here too early."

Wade thanked the clerk and walked down to the harbour. He fancied a beer, so he went into a bar facing the waterside. As he sat at the window sipping his beer he decided to send Danilo a text:

Hi danilo, i'm finally in finisterre, though i had a few problems. It was a nice surprise to see maja here, but i was very sorry to hear that you two had split up. She tells me that you are now walking in andalusia. I wish you well. Keep in touch and take care amigo. Wade.

He finished his beer and ate a bocadillo before walking slowly back to the albergue. The hospitalera, who was waiting at the door, hoping for more customers, greeted him as he went in.

"No news from Maja yet," she said before he had time to ask. "But she will come back tonight."

Wade went up to his room and lay on the bed, where he soon fell asleep. When he woke up he was surprised to find that it was getting dark again. Why was he always so tired these days? He went to the bathroom to freshen himself up before going downstairs for a coffee in reception. There was still no news of Maja.

He wondered if Angelina had read his email and if she'd replied to it yet. He sat down at a computer, checked his email account, and sure enough, there was a message from Angelina:

Hi Wade

I'm glad you finally realised that you would like a real relationship and not just a one night stand. But I think I told you before you should not make me the topic of your Camino.

It's too easy to fall for an 'impossible' woman and to give your heart to her because you know beforehand that it won't turn out right. Really opening up would be with someone you like and there is a possibility for a serious relationship — someone nearer your own age.

Be realistic, Wade! You're getting old. Forget this fantasy that you're only about 35..... it's a little ridiculous, isn't it? But maybe you feel that if there's a woman who might get interested, she will come too close, so it's safer to chase after an 'impossible' woman?

You don't need to have a sexless life now, unless that's what you want. But forget about the tricks you used when you were younger — they don't work with your age anyway. I think women will be more interested if you just take your time to build a relationship, and by then you can order some Viagra ;)

It's too difficult to talk about this stuff by email, no?

I'll come over to England to meet your new partner. :)

Take care

Angelina

Wade wondered if Angelina's friends had returned from their holiday in Mallorca and if she had told them about him. He certainly sensed a marked change of tone. Had her friends advised Angelina to forget the fantasy world of the Camino, to distance herself from this old man and to get on with her own life once more, now that she was beginning to feel well again? He didn't know quite what to think, but he didn't feel like writing any sort of reply just then. He shut down the PC and went out.

He walked the short stretch to the bar he had visited on his way back from the lighthouse. It was now early in the evening and just a few people were there, drinking beer and watching football on TV. Wade ordered a beer and sat at a table where he could see the screen. As time passed, more people came in and he began to think about ordering something to eat. He was busy trying to read the menu when he felt a hand on his shoulder. It was Maja. Wade got up and gave her a big hug.

"Hola Wade, I just got back from Muxia. I thought I might find you here. I will just call Pedro to say where we are. He doesn't know yet that I'm back from Muxia and as this will be my last night in Finisterre, I hope he can come too, to say goodbye."

"You're going back to Austria?"

"Not directly. I'm going first to Santiago because I have some things there and I want to see the cathedral again. Then I need to buy a ticket to get back home."

It was noisy in the bar and she went outside for a few minutes to phone Pedro.

"He'll be here in about half an hour," she said when she came back in. "Maybe we can all eat together then?"

Wade ordered a bottle of wine and they chatted about the Camino while waiting for Pedro. Maja talked a lot about Danilo. It was clear that he was very much in her mind, even now.

"Which room do you have at the albergue?" she asked him.

"Number 7, on the second floor. It's a nice room."

"Yes, I know," she said. "That was the room I shared with Danilo until he left. Then I moved downstairs to the dormitory. It's cheaper."

"I was very sorry to hear that you two had split up," said Wade after a pause. He smiled. "I thought you were soulmates."

She looked at him in her direct way with those piercing blue eyes. "You may be right, but it is hard to see a future for us. Danilo is not a Catholic, he is older than me, and it's a long way from Austria to Argentina. Our two countries are very different."

"I know," Wade replied. "But isn't there a saying that true love will find a way?"

There was a pause before she answered. "I think it's too late now. He hasn't called me since he left Finisterre."

When they were joined by Pedro a few minutes later, they ordered their food and another bottle of wine. Pedro was a local man, who had also recently walked the route from Santiago to Finisterre. He looked about sixty, thought Wade, though he claimed to be forty-nine.

They reminisced about the Camino and Maja spoke a lot about Danilo.

"After León, Danilo and I walked separately again for a while. I wanted to be alone and I dropped behind," she told them. "Then later I wanted to be with him again and I walked more than forty kilometres in one day to catch him up."

"Did you ever feel insecure walking alone?" Wade asked.

"No, not really. People you meet on the Camino are good people. But there was one time when I was walking quite fast and this young man came running, yes running, with a heavy backpack, to catch up with me. Then he walked with me, flirted with me and after maybe just two hours he tried to kiss me. Really! After just two hours. With Danilo, it was two weeks before he kissed me."

"Where was the young man from?" asked Pedro.

"That's the amazing thing about it," said Maja. "He was from Argentina too, but it was Danilo I wanted."

Wade remembered the night he had spent making music with those young guys at the albergue in Vegas, and the young Argentinian he had walked with for a while the following morning."

"I think I met him too," said Wade. "Was his name Enrique?"

"Yes, that's right."

They had finished eating, but the wine was still flowing. When Pedro began to roll a cigarette, Maja asked him to roll one for her as well.

"I didn't know you smoked," said Wade, somewhat surprised.

"Only now and then. It's usually when I drink alcohol," said Maja.

The two went outside to smoke and Wade sat alone at the table. Maybe he could do something to help Maja and Danilo find each other again. He decided to send Danilo a short text:

Danilo, if you want maja, send her a message now!

The reply came back almost instantaneously… or was it a reply?

Wade, hi this is danilo. How are you? It's good to hear about you. Have you talked with maja? How is she? I've got a little worry with your sms. Reply me at my mobile number. thanks.

It took Wade a few seconds before he realised what had happened. Danilo was replying to his text from the day before. Their messages must have crossed. Maja could return at any moment, so he quickly sent another text to Danilo:

She is fine but contact her now.

Then another:

Did you get it? Act now amigo!

Maja and Pedro were still smoking outside, but Pedro came in a few moments later.

"Maja just received a phone call," he said.

When she came back into the bar, Maja's lovely face was a picture of joy. Danilo had contacted her, he would hire a car, they would meet up in Madrid.

"It's amazing! We were just talking about him, then he called me. It must be telepathy."

Wade could only agree, though he didn't say that the telepathy appeared to be between himself and Danilo.

Back at the albergue after saying a fond goodbye to Maja, who would be leaving early in the morning on the first bus to Santiago, Wade went to his room and sent a final text to Danilo:

Great! I am happy you two can come together again. What can i say to you both? I wish you love! Er... maja doesn't know i contacted you, so don't tell her. I wish you both every happiness. Wade

Shortly afterwards Danilo's reply came through.

Wade, muchas gracias!! Ok, I say nothing to maja about your sms. You are a good friend. I wish you buen camino always. Danilo.

*

Wade was up early in the morning in time to say goodbye to Maja. He had slept badly during the night, thinking for hours about Angeline's last message. Then, after Maja left, he helped himself to a cup of coffee from the machine at the albergue, before sitting down at the computer to compose an answer to Angelina's email:

Hi Angelina

Wow! You've certainly brought me down to earth again, though I was already on my way back from the alternative world of the Camino – the 'parallel universe' as you once called it.

I think you were really a bit hard on me. I opened up to you because I had fallen for you, not because it was impossible. It was a feeling I'd almost forgotten. There was nothing 'safe' about it. Whether or not it could turn into something real didn't play a role at the time. You broke down a barrier I had built up against having any intimate relationship with a woman ever again, but it was really only afterwards that I could sense, sometimes, how impossible it was.

When I came to the Camino my goal had nothing directly to do with sex. I wanted to review my life at this critical stage, maybe work out a plan of action for the time that remains to me and, above all, try to find my God. Then when I met you I was confronted with thoughts both of sex and a new relationship. I never pretended to be younger than I am to anybody I met on the Camino. I know many guys (and women too) tell lies about their age in order to give themselves a better chance with the opposite sex. I did it myself years ago in Greece.

The trouble was, that in myself I didn't feel any older than the other guys on the Camino, so I played the same game But you're right, I suppose I didn't really expect success.

I've heard it said that the Camino gives you what you need, not what you want. I've often thought about what that really means. When I started, it was to be a search for my God, but instead, it became a vain attempt to recapture a time that had passed. The time of my youth. This was what I wanted, but what I got was a lesson showing me that time is an arrow pointing ahead - not backwards. It wasn't until Santiago that I finally realised this.

Of course, I would have liked a more intimate relationship with the right woman. Unfortunately for me, the right woman was you. I would love to see you again and you are always welcome to come and stay at my home. Bring a friend too, if you like. But don't wait until I have a new partner, that may never happen.

With love

Wade x

After sending the email, he closed down the computer. He wanted to take a final look at Finisterre before packing his backpack for the last time. He entered a bar near the harbour and sat at a table by the window with a view towards the sea. Then, after a leisurely breakfast, he strolled back to the albergue. He looked at his watch. There was still plenty of time to go online and maybe look at his Facebook page.

As he opened his home page, he noticed that someone had sent him a 'friend request'. It was from someone called Eve Dawson. Wasn't that the mysterious American woman who had been trying to contact him by email? Then, when he saw her 'profile picture' he caught his breath. It was like stepping back in time as long-hidden memories re-emerged. It was an old black and white photo, but not of Eve Dawson. A pretty girl in school uniform and a young man of about thirty were gazing into each other's eyes, and Wade recalled the picture had been taken in a photo booth at Earl's Court underground station nearly forty years before. It was the only photo ever taken of him and Amy together. After a few moments hesitation, he clicked on 'confirm', to accept the friend request.

There were a few people waiting for the midday bus to Santiago, but Wade was the only one with a backpack. It occurred to him that this would be the first time in about six weeks that he had gone anywhere other than on foot. In a strange sort of way, it was almost exciting to be travelling on wheels again, though, on the other hand, he felt a certain trepidation at the thought of returning home. Returning to what? To face up to his guilty secret? Who was Eve Dawson and how did she get hold of that picture of Amy? There would be no more hiding – he had to know.

As they drove back to Santiago Wade had little interest in the coastal scenery, lovely as it was. He could only sit and brood on Angelina's final rejection. At the bus station in Noia, where they stopped for a short break, he decided to send Angelina a last text. There was still something he needed to know – something he had a right to know.

Angelina, that night in burgos. Why did you kiss me like that?

He was surprised when her answer came back almost straight away.

Wade, forget me! That night in burgos I just wanted to show you what you'd been missing all those years.

He texted back:

I don't believe you. It was more than that.

A few minutes went by before the driver returned and they all climbed on the bus for the rest of the journey. As Wade took his seat, his phone buzzed.

I guess you're right. There was a warm feeling between us, no? It was quite spontaneous. But the fact is you are too old for me, wade. You must finally accept that. Take care :) A .

He wiped his eyes and sent her a last text:

I'll try, but i'll never forget that moment. W x

The bus took three hours to reach Santiago, where Wade got out at the bus station in the suburbs of the city and checked out the times of onward buses. His flight wasn't due to leave until the evening, so he decided to have a beer and a snack before finally going on to the airport. The bus station café on the upper level was closed, but nearby, at the top of some steps, he could see a small bar. He crossed over to it and went in.

The place was crowded and at first, he couldn't see anywhere to sit. Then, luckily for him, a couple, who had been sitting at a small table in the corner and next to the window, got up and left. Wade quickly sat down and stuffed his backpack in the corner behind his chair. When the waiter came over, he ordered a beer.

A few minutes later, a man in his mid-fifties came in, carrying two large carrier bags full of groceries. He looked weary and sad and possibly a little drunk, Wade thought, but he was smartly dressed and clearly not a vagrant. The man ordered a beer at the bar counter and looked around for somewhere to sit, but there were no vacant tables.

Wade had read that Spanish people were reluctant to share tables in bars unless invited, so he motioned to the man indicating the spare chair at his table. The man sat down, thanking Wade effusively.

"You Inglés?"

"Yes, that's right."

"I am Manuel," said the man, offering his hand.

"My name's Wade."

They shook hands and Manuel began to talk. He spoke mainly Spanish, but with some words of English dropped in now and then, and Wade understood enough to realise that his new acquaintance had major problems with his family and had been drinking to forget.

Eventually, Manuel called the waiter, paid his bill, thanked Wade and shook his hand again. Manuel walked unsteadily to the door, carrying his heavy bags of shopping and went outside. Wade was alarmed to see him lurching towards the long flight of stone steps which led down to the street below. He had a bag in each hand and could not use the handrail for support. He took the first two steps before falling – luckily backwards onto his behind – and he just sat there helplessly on the hard steps, his bags of shopping still in his hands.

Wade rushed outside, where a woman was already trying to help Manuel to his feet. Together they guided him, half-carrying him, down all the steps to the street below.

"He lives near here," said the woman. "He will be all right now."

Before going further, Manuel put down his bags for a moment and gave Wade a big hug. Then he spoke to the woman, thanked her too, and lurched off.

"He says you are a good man," said the woman. "A very good man."

Wade returned to the bar, finished his beer and asked the waiter for his bill.

"There is nothing to pay," said the waiter. "Your friend paid for everything before he left."

Wade left the bar and went down to the bus station, where he took off his backpack and sat down on a bench opposite the bay for the airport buses. There were a few more minutes to wait. He considered what Manuel had said about him. Was it true? Was he a good man without realising it? Of course, he hadn't actually rediscovered the faith he once had as a child, but maybe in a way, he had come nearer to his God – the indefinable spirit of the universe. In any case, he had finally accepted his age and would not chase shadows any more. There would be no more disruptive thoughts about Angelina.

After a few moments he became aware of a familiar figure sitting next to him – it was Diego of course.

"I wondered if I'd see you again," said Wade.

"This will be the last time," said his old friend. "That is unless you come back to Santiago one day – you still have to continue your spiritual search."

"I know, but at least I'm making some progress at last."

Diego was silent for a few seconds before he spoke again.

"Yes, I believe you are. You are finally ready to face your past, but you are still vulnerable, with your penchant for young women."

"I'm over that now."

"Are you? Don't be too sure. My advice is to regard them as your daughters, or granddaughters, remember your age and stay vigilant," Diego said.

Then, with a smile, he simply faded away in the direction of the old city, just as the bus was arriving.

When he got to the airport, Wade couldn't help noticing how few people there were. The modern terminal building was large enough to accommodate vast crowds of travellers, but clearly, the traffic was seasonal. There were very few people returning home after the Camino now, in mid-December, but he could imagine the hordes who would be there in the summer months.

He was wearing several layers of clothing and his jacket pockets were stuffed full of smaller, heavier items, in order to keep the weight of his backpack under the limit allowed by the airline for cabin bags. It wasn't particularly comfortable and he looked forward to taking off his heavy jacket on the plane. Otherwise, he viewed the coming flight with some trepidation, remembering the trauma of his arrival in Spain some seven weeks earlier. Seven weeks in which so much had happened.

As he waited in the departure lounge, there was an airport announcement about his flight. Owing to problems on another route, it would be subject to a two-hour delay. Wade sighed. This meant they wouldn't arrive in the UK until late at night.

The plane was not full and he was relieved to have been allocated a window seat, where he could rest his head against the fuselage of the plane, and maybe get a little sleep without the fear of nodding off on some stranger's shoulder. He stuffed his backpack and jacket in the overhead locker, with difficulty, before sitting down and fastening his seatbelt. There were the usual safety demonstration and a string of announcements from the cabin crew.

"...Please ensure that all mobile phones are turned off or set to flight mode..."

Wade realised that he hadn't turned off his mobile, but it was in one of his jacket pockets, stuffed in the overhead locker, and nobody was going to call him anyway.

"...Cabin lights will be dimmed for take-off. This is normal practice when flying in the hours of darkness."

He looked through the porthole. Only the lights of the airport shone through the blackness outside, while inside the plane the cabin lights were dimmed. Wade closed his eyes, waiting nervously for the surge of power that signalled take-off, feeling the pressure of the plane's acceleration along the runway pushing him in the back, until at last he sensed that they were in the air and climbing. He looked briefly through the porthole again, seeing the lights of Galicia fading below, then closed his eyes and hoped that he might sleep. He was so very tired...

...At first, everything was totally black, then gradually in the gloom, he began to sense that he was lying on a bed. Ahead of him and to the right was the doorway, to the left was the window. It seemed familiar – he was in his old room on the second floor at the Albergue Cabo da Vila. He watched anxiously as the door slowly opened to reveal a ghostly, hooded figure, wearing a long, flowing translucent robe which reached to the floor as it floated into the room, approaching nearer and nearer to where he lay. A white, shining face with piercing blue eyes looked down, seeming to mock him, and he realised that the Angel of Death in the form of a young woman had come for him. He tried to speak, but no words came. He tried to move, but he couldn't. The ghostly figure hovered directly over him, her robe billowing outwards and upwards revealing her long, pale, slender legs. She descended slowly, her flowing robe gradually covering his head and everything was growing dark again…

"No!" he screamed, as the plane landed heavily on the runway, jolting him awake and startling his fellow passengers. Wade was clutching at his chest, his white face lined with pain, his forehead covered in a cold sweat, but through the suffering, he realised he had overcome his demon and eluded the Angel of Death for the moment at least. By the time the plane had taxied to a halt at the terminal, an ambulance was already waiting to pick him up.

9. TO THE TRUTH

He had spent the first couple of days following his admission to hospital in the Coronary Care Unit. He had been very tired, too tired to think clearly. Maybe it was something to do with all the medication? He really had no idea. Both his children had been over from Germany to see him, so they must have thought it was serious, and his daughter had arranged to stay in London for a few more days to get his flat ready for his return.

Then, on day three, he was transferred to a ward. He was feeling less tired and more able to take an active interest in his surroundings now, and he was anxious to get home as soon as he could. The other patients were not very talkative and the nurses were too busy to chat for long, so apart from his daughter's visits, he was left alone with his thoughts for most of the time. And it was Amy who dominated those thoughts. After all this time, she had escaped from the deep recesses of his mind where he had hidden her and he was ready to face the truth. He wondered if Eve Dawson had replied to his Facebook message? He needed to go online to find out.

Looking back at his first real encounter with Amy, it had been not unlike his experience on the plane before the start of the Camino. But how had it all started?

He recalled how he had gone to pieces, at least emotionally, after Tamsin left him. At that time he had been teaching maths at a co-educational grammar school in West London and it had been a struggle to keep on top of his job, but at least it had taken his mind off the loneliness of his private life. Then, one day, with half-term looming, he volunteered to accompany a group of 'A' level pupils on a class trip to Paris.

"Miss Thorpe will be in charge officially," the headmaster told him. "In fact, the Paris visit is her idea. It won't be a big group – there aren't that many pupils doing 'A' level French and not all the parents can afford it anyway. The girls are civilised enough, but the boys can be a bit noisy if they're not kept in check, so I want a male teacher to go too."

In the event, there were only a few pupils on the trip and one, in particular, had taken Wade's interest – a pretty girl with shoulder length fair-hair, blue eyes and a shy smile. Her name was Amy, originally from New Hampshire, the daughter of an American businessman based in London.

The time in Paris passed without incident, but on arrival at the airport, for the journey back to London, they discovered that their flight had been cancelled. After a delay, they were put on another flight that had some seats available, but the original reservations no longer applied and Wade took an aisle seat, next to Amy. Had it been by chance or design? Looking back, he was no longer certain after such a long time – nearly forty years.

What he did remember was the turbulence of the flight as they approached their destination, with some frightened passengers crying out in alarm. Amy, looking at him with nervous eyes, had touched his arm hesitantly. He had taken her hand in his, and they had continued to hold hands until the plane came to a standstill at the terminal.

He had not really noticed Amy before the trip to Madrid. She had never been in any of his classes and it was a large school. But then, after the half-term holiday, he had seen her everywhere – hanging out in the corridor between classes, drinking coffee with her friends in the school canteen, waiting at the bus stop after school. Why had he never seen her before? Was she waiting for him? Was he looking for her?

He often stayed late on Fridays, to plan his lessons for the following week – he didn't like taking work home with him. One Friday after school, as he came out of the staff room, he met Amy in the corridor just as she emerged from the school library with a couple of books under her arm. There was nobody else around. She had clearly been waiting for him and in her apparent embarrassment dropped the books. He had picked them up, looked into her clear blue eyes, and promptly invited her out for a coffee. That was how it had all started.

Wade was interrupted in his reverie by the arrival of a nurse to take his blood pressure, pulse and temperature, all of which she recorded on a clipboard attached to the foot of the bed. He liked this particular nurse. She was less hectic than some of the others and had a sense of humour.

"Er... does the hospital have any internet facilities? You know, an internet café or something like that for the patients?"

She laughed. "Young man, this is a hospital and not a hotel. You'll have to wait till you get home for all that."

"And when do you think that will be?"

"What's the matter? Don't you like it here? You'll have to ask the doctors about when you can go home, but we need the beds so we won't keep you any longer than necessary."

After the nurse had left, Wade's thoughts returned to Amy. From the beginning, he had been aware of the risks posed by their relationship. They had taken care to avoid being seen together at school, keeping their liaisons to the weekends, and his small flat in Putney had provided their love nest. It was here they had made plans for a future together once Amy left school – a dream that became a nightmare one Monday morning when Wade was summoned to the headmaster's study.

"Whatever possessed you, man? You know the rules here. Relationships between teachers and pupils are taboo."

"I know, but she's already eighteen and..."

"Like hell she is! She's younger than the rest of them in her class."

"But I thought…"

"You didn't think Wade, that's the problem. The girl's father's not only a governor of the school but also a wealthy benefactor and a strict moralist. He'd have your guts for garters if he could, I can tell you. When he discovered that… how shall I say it… that intimate letter you wrote to Amy, he made her tell him everything."

"It was private. It wasn't his letter to read."

"That's not the point. Fact is he's read it, he's withdrawn Amy from the school and he wants you out." He paused a moment before continuing. "You're a good teacher, Wade, and I don't like to see you wrecking your career like this. I suggest that you resign, then I don't have to sack you. In the meantime, you're suspended from all duties."

Wade had been stunned. It had all happened so suddenly. Why had he never asked Amy her age? But it didn't make any difference. He had gone back to Putney in a daze, hoping against hope that she would contact him.

There was a noise and a flurry of activity in the far corner of the ward, where a screen was being quickly erected around the bed next to the entrance doors. The white-faced old man who had occupied the bed had looked terrible all day. Wade could hear voices talking quietly behind the screen, almost whispering. After a time he saw that the doors were open and the old man's bed was being pushed out of the ward. It was covered over. Then the screen was removed and there was an empty space where the bed had been. Wade thought of the old man with the white haggard face.

Had he died with regrets at things he had done or left undone? Had he been ready for death when it came?

It was in the evening, after lights out, that Wade's thoughts returned to Amy. He had to see this through.

A tearful Amy had called him from a phone box in the evening of that fateful last day at school.

"I'm calling from a pay phone, so I can't speak for long. I daren't use the phone at home and if my father notices that I've gone out, he'll get suspicious. I'm so sorry for all this, Wade. I should have taken more care with your love letter."

"No, Amy darling, I'm to blame. But perhaps we can work something out if we—"

"Wade, listen, please. I can't talk now. I'm being sent back to the States tomorrow afternoon on the 16:30 PAN AM flight to New York. They're sending me to live with my grandma for the time being. Mother's dropping me off at the airport, but she won't be staying to see me off. Wait for me near the airline desk and—"

There was a ticking sound before the phone went dead. Amy had run out of coins to extend the call.

The next day Wade travelled to Heathrow to see Amy one last time before her flight to New York. He waited near the airline desk until she arrived and they clung together in a tender embrace. When it was time for her to leave, she handed him a piece of paper.

"You can write to me at this address," she said, with tears shining in her eyes.

Then he watched, as she went through passport

control until she finally disappeared from view.

On his arrival back home, Wade had written some verses and enclosed them in an envelope to send to Amy at the address she had given him. He had kept a copy for himself and had read the verses again and again over the next weeks and months until he knew them off by heart.

Wade was suddenly disturbed by the sound of the man in the next bed getting up and shuffling off to the toilets. Someone else on the other side of the ward was snoring like a tractor. It was a bit like an albergue on a bad night. He knew he wouldn't get to sleep before dawn and he wished he had accepted the sleeping pill the nurse had offered him. He occupied his mind by trying to remember those verses he had written to Amy after she left. As he whispered the lines softly to himself, the tears came.

How I remember that last day,
Those few sad hours before you left.
The sun shone sweetly
And the air was bright,
But my heart was blind to beauty
And my eyes too full of tears
To see the light.

The morning passed in an electric quiet
Where words meant nothing
And the iron fist of fear clenched close.

I hoped that I could see it through
Without unmanly weakness
Or a trembling plea
For you to stay

The final airport hour before your flight,
That was the worst.
I would have wept too,
But my heart was past crying,
My grief engrained
Too deep to burst.

And then a state of limbo
When I saw you through the screen -
I could see but not touch,
Could not hear, could not speak -
Till with a wave you vanished
As if you'd never been.

I went up to the roof
And saw through misted eyes
The gleaming jets rush down the runway
And away.
But which was yours, I knew not
As they climbed into the skies.

Just that you were gone
And there was no turning back.
The day was done.

He had never received a reply from Amy to this, or to any of the subsequent letters he had written, and he had never seen her again.

*

Almost the first thing he did, when he got back home from the hospital, was to switch on his computer. Above all, he wanted to see if Eve Dawson had sent a message following his acceptance of her friend request. However, he had to curb his impatience a little longer while the machine prompted him to install numerous updates before he could use it effectively.

Finally, he was able to log in to his Facebook account. Sure enough, the mysterious Eve had sent him a long private message, which he read several times:

Dear Wade,

I hardly know how to begin, but I think I should tell you right away that the schoolgirl you loved in London, all those years ago, died in a car crash last year. I should also tell you that Amy was my mother, though I didn't know this until I was in my twenties.

You see, when I was a baby I was given free for adoption and I always believed that my adoptive parents were my birth parents. It was only after they died that I discovered they were not my 'real' parents at all, though they had always felt real to me. I was single at the time and it was unsettling to be alone in the world. Then I got pregnant and I felt the need to find my roots, if only for the sake of the child. For this reason, I began the search for my birth mother.

I finally tracked Amy down. She was married to an older man, living a comfortable life in Miami, and I guess at first she wasn't too keen to face the past. But as we got to know each other better, we became closer, and eventually, she told me all about your affair in London and how she had been sent back to the States by her domineering father, with strict instructions not to contact you.

Amy had discovered she was pregnant when she got back to New York, and when her father found out, he insisted that her baby be put up for adoption. If she hadn't agreed to this, he had threatened to make big trouble for you, Wade. He didn't want his only daughter to be tied to some impoverished teacher in London. Amy succumbed to her father's control, and after I was adopted she picked up her life as if her affair with you and my birth had never happened. She went to high school, married well, settled down and almost forgot about me. I say 'almost' because she never had any other children, and there were times when I think she regretted this.

After Amy and her husband died in the car crash, I was left as her closest relative. When I was going through her personal effects I came across some letters and a photo in a large envelope. The photo looked like it had been taken in one of those automatic photo booths and it showed a pretty girl in school uniform and a good-looking guy of around 30. Of course, the girl was Amy and the guy just had to be you.

The letters were from you, written over a period of several months after she had returned to New York. Maybe I shouldn't have read them, but I did. It was clear from your *letters that Amy had never replied to any of them. But it was also clear to me that she had never really forgotten you – or why had she kept the letters all those years?*

I resolved to try and find you. Of course you were no longer in Putney after all this time, so I started with your mother's address in north London (you mentioned it in one of your letters to Amy) only to find out you had sold the house after your mother died. The new owners didn't know where you'd moved to, but they were able to give me the name of the law firm who acted for you when you sold them the house. They told me they would pass on my email address to you, but I never heard any more. Then finally I hit on the idea of trying to find you through Facebook and – well, you know the rest.

Where we go from here is up to you. really. There's a lot more I could tell you, but I realise you might not want to dig up the distant past. However, I hope you will at least write and let me know how you feel.

Yours

Eve

Wade thought long and hard about Eve's message. It was mind-blowing. Eve was his daughter – maybe a reluctant one, but his daughter, nonetheless. His whole Camino experience had, in some mysterious way, prepared him for this moment.

10. THE PORTICO OF GLORY

The old city was much more crowded than he remembered it, but in spite of mass tourism the aura of spirituality and faith, in and around the cathedral, had been preserved. Now, after years of restoration, boarded up and hidden behind scaffolding, the Portico of Glory had been revealed in all its... well, 'glory' he supposed was the only word to describe it. He remembered the slight air of disappointment, at the end of his Camino five years before, to find scaffolding on the main facade, with the traditional pilgrim access to the cathedral blocked in order to accommodate the restoration works. Not only that, but the famed Botafumeiro had been out of action that day, and he smiled to himself as he recalled Philippe's joke at the time about walking two thousand kilometres for nothing.

Now, with the Portico of Glory open again, he would have an opportunity to finally finish Camino the traditional way, to appreciate the lessons it had taught him and to give thanks for what it had given him.

He waited near the middle of the square, facing the cathedral, straining his eyes to look toward the crowds of arriving pilgrims coming through the tunnel on the left, at the culmination of their Camino.

He was leaning heavily on his stick. His arthritic knees were hurting and it had been hard enough to walk the short distance from his hotel. This would be his last Camino – the short stretch from here, through the Portico of Glory and into the cathedral. Someone else, someone he loved, had walked the rest of the way for him.

His mobile buzzed. It was the same phone he had taken on his original Camino. He took it from his pocket and then nearly dropped it as he fumbled to find his glasses. Finally, he was able to read the message.

"Arrived santiago. Porta do camino. With you in a few minutes. A xxx"

"Waiting for you. Xxx," Wade texted back.

He continued to gaze fixedly toward the tunnel until, suddenly, he spotted her. She was walking with a group of other young people, but when she saw him she waved, gave her backpack to one of her companions, and ran towards him. How lovely she looked, with her long fair hair swept back from her forehead and her blue eyes shining. There was no mistaking the resemblance to her grandmother.

"Hi, grandpa. It's awesome to have you here to meet me."

He gave her a big hug. "Amy, I wouldn't have

missed this moment for worlds."

Wade glanced up to the central gable of the cathedral facade, between the two main towers, where a statue of St James as a pilgrim was silhouetted against the sky.

"Thank you, Diego," he said simply.

THE END

ABOUT THE AUTHOR

Michael Small taught English as a Foreign Language in Germany for many years until his retirement. Some time later, after walking the Camino de Santiago de Compostela, he resolved to fulfil an ambition and write his debut novel – *Waiting For Amy*.

These days he lives in Devon, by the sea; but he is a frequent visitor to northern Spain and Germany, where he has friends and family.

37534107R00152

Printed in Poland
by Amazon Fulfillment
Poland Sp. z o.o., Wrocław